THE CLOUD MESSENGER

ALSO BY AAMER HUSSEIN

Fiction
Mirror to the Sun
This Other Salt
Turquoise
Cactus Town: Selected Stories
Insomnia
Another Gulmohar Tree

Editor
Kahani: Short Stories by Pakistani Women

The Cloud Messenger

Aamer Hussein

TELEGRAM

ISBN: 978-1-84659-089-4

Copyright © Aamer Hussein 2011

This first edition published in 2011 by Telegram

A full CIP record for this book is available from the British Library.
A full CIP record for this book is available from the Library of Congress.

Printed and Bound by CPI Mackays,
Chatham, ME5 8TD

TELEGRAM
26 Westbourne Grove, London W2 5RH
www.telegrambooks.com

Contents

My beloved puts on a garment of clouds today ...

From the Sur Sarang (Rain Song)
of Shah Abdul Latif

I

A Flute Died

I heard two gulls cry at dawn today.

Why do they come to town in summer, so far from their body of water? I asked you that day when they circled over our heads as we drank coffee on the cobbled pavement by the canal. Remember? It's a sign of coming rain, you said. They fly inland when it rains. But only a few days later somebody told me they weren't seabirds at all: just scavengers that visited cities in search of refuse from dustbins.

The day I heard the gulls cry my friend broke her flute in the place that once was rainless. The flute had been her companion, her voice when she couldn't speak. The flute had travelled with her across two oceans. For hours she tried to fix it, but she'd forgotten how. She wept for a day. It had rained all day and night for a week before the flute died, and often there was no light.

The cut-off flute laments and the wounded woman wails, Latif of Bhit said. That one remembers being one with the tree, this one longs for her beloved.

One day, when we loved each other, you said a falcon flew out of a book and perched on your shoulder. You couldn't keep her. You let her fly away. The perfect falcon from a poem by Rumi.

In the rainless place, the clouds before sunset took on the shapes of birds. Remembering them now, I can see the falcons. The flight of swans. And the gulls.

When my friend mourned her flute I told her how, just a few weeks before, I'd complained to you about a recalcitrant and loving heart. It's a wild, wild dog that feeds on us from the inside, I'd said: it won't be tamed.

My friend said: Sometimes I feel you write my words. As if you've stolen them from me.

That afternoon, sitting again on that cobbled pavement by the canal, I asked a poet if he would call the heart a beast or a falcon.

The swan dives into limpid water to seek pearls. Cranes and gulls are content with dirty water. Latif says, look just once at the swans: you'll never be friends again with the cranes.

Why did your perfect falcon fly? Why is my shoulder empty?

The rain came down hard. We took shelter under a tree.

My friend said, I want you to write a story that's rain-coloured: rain-grey, rain-blue.

You walk away in the rain. You say someone is waiting. I won't call out your name. Won't see you turn, look back. They say you shouldn't stop someone who's leaving. And never call out to them from behind.

When my friend's flute died she laid it to rest in

its black silk case but didn't bury it. It gave you its voice, I told her. The clouds carried my messages to her, from the city of my present to the place where her flute died.

As grass and straw, being cut, complain, Latif says, suddenly comes the beloved's sigh of pain.

I want to write my story. With the sound of the rain in it. The sound of rain on leaves and grass. And the flute's lament.

My friend said: Sometimes I feel you write my words. As if you stole them from me. Or you took them from the sea or the city of our birth.

And I tell you then: The heart's a bird. Or a cloud in the shape of a bird. An unwritten letter in its cry. It's not a perfect falcon. Nor even a swan diving for pearls. No. It's a gull, in search of sustenance. Or rain.

II

Rain Songs

What is a cloud, after all, but smoke, air and water?
What are my messages, to be silenced by the vanity of sending them by cloud?
I am a passionate lover, eager to reach my beloved.

From the Meghaduta *of Kalidasa*

I

Father and daughter shared memories of a distant place they had lived in once. They would talk for hours about Hyde Park and Stanmore, Selfridges, Bill and Ben the Flowerpot Men and Noddy, crumpets and strawberries with cream. It was, to Mehran and his younger sister Sara, insufferably exotic (though they didn't know the word yet). At the same time, Mehran and Sara felt excluded by their tales, and even provincial. Mehran was the second child, the only boy in a family of three. They lived in Karachi, a hot city, where they ate oranges, bananas, mangoes, papaya and custard apples, knew only the desert and the sea, couldn't imagine what strawberries or crumpets tasted like; milk and cream made them sick. And if their mother decided to join her husband and her oldest daughter Sabah in remembering that winter day when she would walk on a pond sheathed in thin ice and fallen in, Mehran would feel even more excluded. Since his only picture of snow was what he saw on Christmas cards, in a place that hardly knew rain, snow was as strange to him as chimneys and Santa Claus.

Mehran's father received the gauzy sheets of *The Times* every two or three days, and he would discuss ballets and pantomimes with Sabah: one of their most vivid recollections was of being taken to see Russian dancers perform *Swan Lake* at the Royal Opera House. (For Mehran, entertainment, in those times without television, meant films, puppet shows, amateur dramatics, fancy dress parties and fairs.) Father also had letters from abroad with pictures of the queen on their stamps.

They saw the queen in 1960. She wore a yellow-petalled hat and waved to hundreds of bystanders from a car. Sabah was taken to meet her; Sara and Mehran weren't, too little as they were at four and five.

'Does she rule over us, then?' Mehran wanted to know.

'No,' his mother said.

'Why', he asked, 'do we call her a queen?'

'She's the Queen of England,' he was told.

Was England in London? Was London in Pakistan, or in India? Mehran knew India was far away, because getting there required a drive to the airport, a wait in a lounge, a trip on a noisy plane, and a long, long drive into town once they reached Bombay.

'No, it isn't, it's much further than India, very far away.'

On that, at least, they could agree.

In England, Mehran's mother had been asked if she was a princess (which she was, in a way, though she didn't like to be called that) or a movie star. (One day, she came across Louis Jourdan shooting for a film with Leslie Caron. She asked them for an autograph; they took out their pens and asked for hers.) At home, she seemed quite normal, though she was different from most people's mothers. People often gasped at her beauty when they saw her; she sang very well, and frequently drove her little car up one-way streets.

Sabah had every Enid Blyton book that had ever been published, and inevitably Mehran read them as he made the transition from picture books to more grown-up tales of adventure. But though he couldn't understand the food they talked about – marmite and potted shrimps – the Famous Five and their picnics seemed very adventurous in comparison with the sedate family outings he knew, where adults and children drove off together to the seaside or some green place. The thrill of the Five's midnight feasts was something he couldn't replicate, as getting up to raid the fridge after midnight seemed an exceedingly tame act when the fridge was stocked especially for the children with apples and pears, and chocolate and cheese, and some hapless servant might rise and rush to ask Mehran and Sara what they needed, thinking they had been underfed at dinner.

Reading about England made Mehran no more curious than he was about China or Estonia. (The first foreign city he visited, at Christmas, when he was nearly eleven, was Rome, which he had wanted to see: when the chance came at the end of that Italian trip to visit London or Beirut, he preferred to go to Beirut because it was on the way home and he had heard London was freezing.) But Andersen and the Brothers Grimm and the narratives in the Old Testament and the Qur'an he loved, up to and beyond graduating to *The Iliad*, *The Odyssey* and the *One Thousand and One Arabian Nights*.

Without knowing the word, Mehran knew when he was about five that his father was a permanent expatriate. Born in Karachi, Mehran's father had grown up in many other places. As a teenager he had been sent off alone in a ship to England, where he studied for several years until, in 1939, his own father's anxieties about the war took him away. He had, when independence diminished his family's lands and fortunes, become the director of a company that sold many fine varieties of rice to Middle Eastern countries, and other commodities to other places. He travelled so frequently that the family joke was to define his destinations by days of the week: Monday was Beirut, and Sunday – the day of rest – was, of course, reserved for London, which remained his favourite holiday destination. And though he was very much a part of Karachi – it was hard to imagine the city without him – when he was with them he was always dreaming of other places.

Mehran's mother was more immersed in the life of her husband's native city than he ever seemed to be. Apart from getting the children to school on time, often driving or collecting them herself, then overseeing their homework, there were charities, art exhibitions, fashion shows, diplomatic receptions and concerts. At home, the music lessons twice a week, or the occasional article she was bullied into writing by hand, and dictating over the phone, by an aunt or some importunate friend who worked for *Dawn* or *The Morning News*, kept her busy from morning till, at times, after midnight. Then there were the huge family gatherings they hosted occasionally on Sundays, when Mehran's uncles and aunts and their offspring turned up for enormous meals.

Their mother's expatriation was of another sort. Mehran knew she had moved here as a bride in 1948, from Indore, her birthplace, and gone with his father and Sabah, their infant daughter, to London, two years after; back in Karachi a couple of years before Mehran was born, she had made every effort to recreate, in her gardens, a semblance of the landscape she had left behind in Indore. Mehran had an early memory of the first house they moved to in the late fifties: a truck arriving to plant grass in the barren yard. He could have been inventing it, but he was sure his parents had chosen the house because it was on a hill full of hedges and wild flowering bushes, with soil more fertile than the sand and rock that seemed to make up most of Karachi. And when he said, one day, that he remembered the garden growing green and grassy overnight, his father laughed. ('You weren't far from wrong,' his mother told him many years later. 'The grass was imported from New Zealand; it was the fast-growing kind.')

Try as she might, their mother's Karachi gardens could only create illusions of her native place: the air and the water were different. She had grown up in a region where vegetation was lush, trees very tall, and there were wells and running water at every corner. The gardens she made combined natural resources – bougainvillea, cacti, frangipani, guava – with imported orchids and roses. The search for home was a question of green motifs: grassy beds and shadowy places. When Mehran was six she moved them higher up the hill, to a house where another expatriate had made a garden with terraces, arbours and bowers, and almonds and stunted orange trees in great coral-coloured pots, which probably evoked the greener places she'd left behind.

Mehran's mother was a singer who never made her

art into a profession, though she sang for large gatherings of acquaintances and dignitaries. Her teacher, a maestro of the Delhi school, taught her haunting *raga*s which the children learned from her without great effort as she rehearsed her difficult melodic ornamentations. Some of her songs were poems she had set to music herself; poems by Faiz or Ghalib, or the heart-wrenching lyrics of separation Rani Roopmati had sung for her husband, Baz Bahadur. Other songs were about the rain, as were her stories. She would tell them of the exiled man who asked a cloud to carry messages to his beloved in the city he had left behind, describing the route and the cities over which the cloud would travel. And in Mehran's mind, those cities were always in his mother's native Malwa.

Under the almond tree, playing the *tanpura*, she would sing the words of Amir Khusro, the Songbird of Delhi, words that seemed to echo Kalidasa from another, later age:

Abr o baran o man o yar satadah ba vida
Man juda girya konam abr juda yar juda
Sabza naukhez o gul o bostan sar sabz
Bul bul e ru-e-siyah manda be gulzar juda

The cloud and the rain and my friend and I
     about to say goodbye,
I weep apart, my friend apart, the cloud apart,
The verdant grass, the rose in bloom, the garden
green.

The dark-faced nightingale from the flower
apart.

And in that garden, by another tree – a frangipani
– Sara and Mehran read *The Lady of the Lotus*, a
big and beautifully bound blue volume illustrated
with miniatures in delicate colours, which told the
story of Roopmati, who poisoned herself for love of
Baz Bahadur when predatory Adham Khan came to
claim her favours. Set in Mandu, only a few miles
away from their mother's native place, it reminded
them of Indore and the rainy season.

Sabah, with all the English ways she had acquired
as a little girl in the London she had loved, reached
her teens in the new house in 1962, and studied
in the international milieu of the Convent of Jesus
and Mary, where Sara and Mehran were later sent
at the ages of seven and eight. Two or three times
a year Sabah would have parties in the garden, to
which all her school friends, foreign or local, came
dressed and made up like Hollywood actresses, and
danced till their cars came to take them home at the
Cinderella hour. These girls inhabited some private
city within the city, their own particular teenage
fairground.

But to Mehran's mother the topography of sandy,
stony Karachi, with its tall palm trees and stunted

cacti, felt foreign. And all her children longed for rain as if they were born into intimacy with the rainy season, though they had grown up in this place where the rain was so rare: many of their games involved sprinklers, fountains, tubs and ponds to create illusions of the monsoon.

Of her three children, Mehran at least inherited something of her estrangement from the city's climate. Once when he was three or four there was a three-day downpour and the watermelon patch filled up like a pool, and they bathed with their mother in its tea-coloured water. It must have been May. Sometimes, though, on summer days when the heat was overpowering or dust storms forced the city to shut down for the space of an afternoon, or clouds promised rain for three days at a time and never delivered a drop, their mother would admit she was missing her childhood home. Then Mehran and his sisters would plead with her to make plans for their next journey.

2

It was rare for their mother to leave Karachi without her children in tow. She took them to places they could share with her: unlike London, these were cities Mehran knew well, the only otherwhere he had, and more exciting to him than unknown England or Enid Blyton. There was Bombay, that big, messy city which, like theirs, was by the sea, but in other ways was very different; it grew upwards, and was hemmed in by its waters, whereas in Karachi houses were houses, smallish and detached and enclosed in walled gardens, and the sea that bordered the city was miles and miles away from where they lived. In Bombay they could see the sea from every window in the house.

Mehran had cousins in Bombay, and friends. There were cinemas a few moments' walk or drive away from where they stayed, and a club by a nearby beach. In Karachi they lived a half-hour's drive away from the centre of town; getting to the cinema or the seaside was a long-haul plan, and there was only a little market, called the Nursery, a short walk away from them at the foot of the hill, where everything from marzipan cakes to paperback novels, sanitary towels to sticky toffees, and sharpeners with wiggly 3D figures on them could be had. There was an ice cream parlour called The Dew Drop Inn frequented by the more louche teenagers of the area in their skin-tight clothes, who were known as Teddies; Mehran and his sisters could only drop in if they were in adult company, otherwise they would have to send the driver in to buy them strawberry ice cream cones. No such strictures in Bombay, where cones could be had on every corner. It was as if they had strayed from a still and enclosed world into movement and expansion. Bombay people were louder and freer than they were, but also – at least in comparison with the privileged class – spoke less elegant English, watched Hollywood movies and listened to British pop (the Beatles, the Stones and Sandy Shaw were more in vogue with them in the mid-sixties than American singers) later than Mehran and his friends did; they were still wearing drainpipes when Mehran had migrated to flares.

His mother was always impatient to move on from Bombay to the place she missed most of all: Indore, her home town, which Mehran always mentioned last because it remained, to him, at least, if not to all of his siblings, the most important. There, the passage to another time was complete, but this, rather than calendar time, was the time of fiction, though Mehran only recognised this in his thirties when he became a voracious reader of classic Urdu novels. To them as children, it was a story that they were living rather than reading, but also writing to read later, as if it were a diary, when they were back at home.

Their grandparents' two-storey house, with its red-tiled porch and terraced roof, and its inner courtyard which was the centre of much of their activity, stood in a vast garden of mango, guava and lime trees. There was a well by the outer wall, shadowed by the tallest tree Mehran had ever seen – a eucalyptus. (His mother remembered his grandmother strolling there, telling her beads by the jasmine bushes.)

Mehran's grandfather, the patriarch, had his domain on the ground floor, which was at once drawing room, study and library, where books from east and west sat side by side: *Annals and Antiquities of Rajputana* next to Hawthorne, Fitzgerald's *Khayyam* elbowing Plutarch and an Urdu translation of Firdausi. He also had a room upstairs, overlooking the garden, in which he spent time until an operation left him – that man who had walked several miles a day – unable to walk without great effort. His den was the central room in the front wing of the ground floor, which led into the garden.

To the left of his grandfather's room, if you faced it from the inner courtyard, was his grandmother's realm. She recited Rumi's poems in Persian, knew every one of Khusrau's verses, and spoke the sweetest Urdu in the world; when Mehran was eleven, she untied his tongue by teaching him his language properly. She held court from her four-poster bed, with her books and a few treasured objects beside her. Not averse to certain western innovations if she found them comfortable, she had opted for tradition in her own room. The fine carpet on the floor was always covered by a crisp white sheet, littered with fat cushions on which her children, grandchildren and guests sat around her. The only foreign intrusion in this room was the easy chair, close to the always open door, that she kept there for her husband's frequent incursions into her kingdom. (Once, she said, she was taking her afternoon nap when she thought he entered, sat down and lit a cigarette; she smelled the smoke of perfumed tobacco linger in the air. She didn't hear him leave. A little later, awake now, she saw him come in again. She apologised for not having roused herself before. I wasn't here, he said. Another incident, also in the afternoon, took place when in her sleep she felt his hand play with her silver anklet, and opened her eyes to find no one there.)

In the courtyard was a room that stood apart, like a little pavilion. It was occupied by Mehran's grandmother's sister, another wanderer who moved from town to town depending on the season. She was a widow, and the clan's storyteller. Fiction or fact, you could rely on her to keep the records, or straighten the twist in the tale. Among the romances she told over three afternoon sessions – she always stopped before sunset, as she held onto the storytellers's tradition that travellers lost their way if you told a story when light and darkness met – were 'The Prince with the Needles in his Eyes', 'The Patient Princess', and the story of Prince Benazir and his escape from the Bad Fairy Mahrukh who held him captive, and his redeeming love for the princess, Badremunir, who rescued him.

The grandmother's youngest brother Rafi, Mehran and his sisters were told, had published a book of very beautiful stories. Mehran's mother and her siblings knew him as Mamu Mian, the charming, elegant poet and storyteller who died very young, when Mehran's mother was about thirteen.

Until Rafi's generation, Persian had been the family language, and he and his sisters and brothers remained bilingual. Mehran's grandmother was the first in the family to begin to write in Urdu; she submitted poems, articles on conduct and essays on religion to a journal called *Saheli*. When, in 1913, Mehran's grandmother married the young chieftain from Kathiawar, a radical who had turned his back on family wealth to become a teacher and housemaster, she gave up writing to bring up her children, all of whom inherited her love of the arts and their father's intellectual bent.

Mamu Mian was, Mehran's mother recalled, a very frequent visitor to Indore in the thirties. He had begun to write at a very early age, and was a regular contributor to a journal called *Sarosh*, in which Mehran's aunts and mother read his stories. By now, the family communicated mostly in Urdu; when they were visiting an aunt who addressed them in Persian, they responded in Urdu and she rebuked them in Farsi: '*Tuf be shoma! Farsi faramosh kardid.*'*

To the left of Grandfather's domain was Mehran's uncle's apartment, a little bastion of modernity within the timelessness of the family home. Furnished practically and smartly, it was remarkable, above all, for the range and number of books it held: in the bedroom, novels by Nabokov, Murdoch and Barth; in the study, volumes of Indian history, where, at the age of thirteen, Mehran read enough about ancient and medieval times to get a high mark in an exam without studying the set texts at his new school which was in the south, so far away that it seemed to be another country.

Mehran's uncle was a historian, whose voluminous research in Indian history, from ancient times

* 'Shame! You've forgotten your Farsi!'

to the establishment of the Mughal Empire, was a corrective response to colonialist texts. Six feet tall, with prematurely silvered hair, he was as handsome as a god or a movie idol – of the Hollywood, not the Bollywood, variety.

Mehran and his sisters had to switch languages here, practising Urdu grown threadbare from disuse with various members of the extended clan who would have found their English chatter a frivolous affectation.

The city was surrounded by forest, ravines and rivers. Hunting duck and deer was a frequent pastime for women and men alike. (In her teens, Mehran's mother shot a crocodile; her older sister bagged a tiger.) In Indore, Mehran and his sisters seemed to go back in time to the contingent rules and regulations of a more generous and noble era which, with all its sometimes welcome strangeness, had always been familiar from their parents' ways. But if, in Karachi, Mehran had tried to tell friends about riding elephants on wedding days, or shooting deer in bandit-infested forests, they would have thought it all not only exotic but far less believable than an Enid Blyton story.

In Indore, life's pace was tranquil, and for a city child, restorative. Mehran read, ate fresh fruit from the garden and honey from a farm on some family member's estate. Occasionally they drove to the centre of town. It was there that he discovered, at the age of nine, the numerous translations of Indian classics,

The Ramayana and Kalidasa's plays and poems, 'Shakuntala' and 'Meghaduta' (the story of the cloud messenger) among them, that one could buy in cheap local editions from a bookshop called Rupayana, near the India Coffee House where, after book-shopping, Mehran could regale himself on crisp *dosa* washed down with hot South Indian coffee.

Ketan, the neighbour's son, who taught Mehran to ride a bicycle and took him to see Hindi films on warm afternoons, remained his best friend for ten years, though Mehran only ever saw him for two or three weeks a year, and would almost forget him when he went away. But every year Ketan would be there, in the courtyard, on his bicycle, loudly calling out his name; Mehran would go down and take his seat behind him, and they would ride down the lanes to the centre of town.

(This was the beginning of a significant pattern in Mehran's life. As a child, moving from place to place, he would form significant relationships – with family or friends – only to move on, leaving them behind or carrying them with him as figments of fleeting memory. Later, the pattern would reverse: it was he who, living for a decade in one city with little chance to move away, would meet people who entered his restricted zone to befriend him, elicit some tentative affection and then move away. Mehran came to believe that people – and their affections – were like floating clouds: here one hour, gone the next.)

3

Mehran carried home an adult reading habit, which his Karachi aunt, his father's sister, indulged by giving him *My Cousin Rachel* and *Gone with the Wind* when he was ten – the latter causing him to wake up at night in a panic, thinking the Yankees were coming, especially when, later that year, war broke out between India and Pakistan. His older sister Sabah had always been distant, as if she belonged to another world; now his younger sister Sara, too, walked into a world of hopscotch and skipping ropes and dolls that was unfamiliar to Mehran, as if forced, by an unwritten rule, to play the game of girl-hood, though they would remain friends and allies in some unspoken way. For Mehran, there was to be no wrestling, boxing or cricket; only tall trees to climb, walks down the hill, and many, many books to read. In that season of *Gone with the Wind*, his mother, who had tried to inculcate in her growing children a taste for Dickens and the Brontë sisters, bought him a handsome edition of *War and Peace*: better an epic than a potboiler, and a racist one at that, she must have thought.

The Karachi aunt lived next door. Widowed young, and childless, she had reinvented herself as a member of parliament, travelled frequently to attend its sessions, and remarried, surreptitiously, a man who lived in Rawalpindi and visited her rarely. The arrangement seemed to suit her solitary ways. When she was at home, she lived alone with a cocker spaniel and two parrots, all given to her by Mehran's father. Her library had everything in it – in expensive hardcover – from Isak Dinesen and Iris Murdoch to Flaubert and Pasternak (chosen, his sister Sabah was convinced, by the Book of the Month Club). Twice a week when she was in town, Mehran was summoned into the aunt's presence to share her supper of soup, grilled chicken and two vegetables, followed by fruit or creamy confections. He was rewarded with a book or two to take away for a week.

Mehran was two or three when the aunt lost her first husband; she had insisted on taking him home with her, away from his parents, to sleep beside her and replace the son she never had. Often Mehran would awaken, in pitch darkness, thirsty, and be too afraid to call out in the night for water. One night, during Ramadan, she decided to sleep in Mehran's parents' house instead, probably for the companionship of breakfast in the pre-dawn hours. He must have been four. He woke up in the dark, in fear, and stumbled out of bed, to the light, where she was at breakfast with his parents and Sabah. When, the next evening, she wanted to take Mehran back to her house, he clung to his mother's legs and refused to go with her. He had heard that she was planning to take him on a trip across the sea. After that day, though she never claimed Mehran as her child again, she did, from time to time, say that he had an impudent double called Wicked Willie Winkie who had taken over the identity of the quiet, gentle boy he was by habit. Mehran and his sisters were taught to give her unstinting affection, since she had no children, and it took Mehran years to realise how very little she had given any of them in return. (Tellingly, the aunt's name was Mahrukh, like the fairy who stole the boy-prince Benazir from his parents as he lay sleeping. But while Prince Benazir was twelve when the fairy abducted him, Mehran was three when his aunt took him away; and he didn't hear the story of Benazir and the Bad Fairy until much later, from his storytelling great-aunt in Indore.)

'When did you first begin to miss Karachi?' Mehran's mother asked him when he was much, much older. 'Not Karachi, but the idea of a city of my own,' was his answer. It was long, long after leaving, when he'd spent half his life away, that he began to excavate the contours of a city sunken in his memory's depths. The house and garden in Indore, on the other hand, had always stayed in his consciousness. But he remembered a trip through Bombay at the age of nine, waiting to go back home while the rain was relentless and his mother was lingering; it was late August, the new term was about to begin, and the time had come for them to leave. Was it his books he missed, or his house and garden? One or two friends, or the way he knew the city centre well enough to guide a driver anywhere he needed to go alone, most frequently a bookshop? (Mehran knew the artery of roads, lanes and byroads around Elphinstone Street, Saddar and Bunder Road, all the cinemas and sweetshops and vendors of fruit and food.)

But Karachi, which had given Mehran his sense of a city's life, was never his only place; perhaps because of that he always felt slightly restless there. Was it the city's rainless climate that made Mehran long for the other homes he knew? Like his parents, he too spent many hours sending cloud messages to other places, messages of longing for something that he knew existed otherwise. There were all the characters from his Indian story he missed: people he loved, but knew only from a respectful distance; in the two or three dense years he spent away from them because of war and strife between the two countries, they became shadowy but remained beloved, like people from a well-loved but half-remembered childhood book: or even more like those leaves or petals placed between the pages of a book, which elicit a twinge of longing but don't immediately remind you of what it was you wanted to save, petal, leaf or page.

When his father finally decided to leave his birthplace to resettle in the rainy country of his youth, Mehran was nearly thirteen. He and his sisters were scattered: Sara and he went to India, to see whether they would be happier, at least for a year or two, in their other monsoon world. Sabah followed their father to England; their mother stayed behind, alone with the Bad Fairy Mahrukh, to wind up two decades of life in Karachi.

For years Mehran never looked over his shoulder at the city he had left behind. Karachi in his twenties and thirties remained a foreign place to him. When he went back he was forty-one, and almost a stranger to the topography of a city he could only recognise in fragments. He didn't contact most of his father's relatives, though the one aunt he did visit forced him to meet some of them. (But what is the loss of a place compared to the grief of losing people? Grandfather, grandmother, aunt, cousin – he took an interminable journey that severed him from all of them. It was only when he heard the news of his grandmother's death that

India called him back in a voice so loud he had to listen. As it would call him back, time after time. But why not count, instead, the ones he saw again, in London or in India – aunt, uncles, cousins, friends – to console him for the ones he'd lost?)

And what did Mehran miss about Karachi in those years after he left, when he hardly ever thought about it? Did he miss his father's English-speaking relatives, with their Cambridge degrees and garrulous ways? They all lived separate lives, in different, distant parts of town, the relatives in Clifton, Bath Island and Defence, Mehran and his family in Shah Abdul Latif Road. Apart from those family Sundays, the two big Eids were the major occasions for the extended clan to get together. That was when Mehran saw the relatives referred to as The Sindhi Cousins, who were gaudier, bawdier, and far more loving then the Karachi clan, with a gift for feasting and a love of music which meant that they invited some renowned singer to perform at every festivity. In Karachi, worship seemed tied to the cycles of the day and the calendar: you prayed when you saw the new moon, which announced the coming of Ramadan and of Eid, as the rising of the light announced the time to commit yourself to the day's fast, and the setting of the sun announced the time to break it with another prayer. So there was, in Mehran's mind at least, a connection between the sky and the seasons and God, who remained an exterior and primordial being. Mehran remembered only one Eid in Indore, which, apart from a visit to the mosque for the men, and special sweets, was as quiet as any other day. His grandmother prayed, without any ceremony, five times a day, as did most of his mother's family. Looking back, Mehran came to see that prayer there had ceased to be a ritual, to become, instead, reflection: an intense and private duty which brought your Maker closer to you than your jugular vein. Now, in London, Mehran often reads from a little book of prayers in a sunlit room where leaves press against the glass.

In Karachi, every rhythm of the day was broken by the telephone. There was no telephone in Indore. You read and you talked and you listened to stories and played in the garden, and in the cool of the night you went for after-dinner walks along the leafy lanes. Then, refreshed, you left. Mehran never felt he would have enough of that life until, in his fifteenth year, he stayed there for two months, and, tired of the rainy season, started to long for sun and the city again. It was as if he was shedding, cell by cell, his reason for belonging. By then he had spent eighteen months in that small town in the southern hills, and tasted the salt of foreign cities – Rome, Naples and Beirut; in leaving behind Karachi, he had said goodbye to the sandy tract between the desert and the sea that was his native place. He knew he would soon be moving on, to live in the rainy city his father and his sister had made their own so many years before, the city he had never seen.

III

A Painted Happiness

And when I paint that loving jealousy
With chalk upon the rock, and my caress
As at thy feet I lie, I cannot see
Through tears that to my eyes unbidden press –
So stern a fate denies a painted happiness

From the Meghaduta *of Kalidasa*

1978

Marco Feliciani was a bit of a lad: spare and sturdy, with amber eyes and chestnut curls, at first glance he looked either petulant or pensive, depending on his mood, until you saw the wry grin on his thin lips. He loved good films, the theatre, food, lots of sex (he said), smoking dope and (very occasionally) getting drunk on beer, red wine or grappa. Sometimes, on a Sunday, he attended Mass at Brompton Oratory. He had travelled all over Asia in his teens, working in Catholic convents in South India and Buddhist monasteries in Thailand. He had got my number from Tina, a Venetian girlfriend of mine he'd met at a party: she said I was someone with whom he might practise his spoken Urdu, and give Italian lessons to in exchange. Though my Italian was quite fluent I didn't want to rebuff him, and vaguely thought the encounter with a future colleague might be interesting. I'd just left a job in a bank where I had worked for a year; at twenty-three, I was about to go back to study something I had always wanted to.

I first met him in the foyer of the Everyman cinema, and wasn't immediately drawn to him. He seemed opinionated and world-weary, though I was soon to discover he was only five months older than I was. Then some chance remark I made in Urdu made him grin and show strong white teeth. We relaxed with each other. After that, there were visits to the cinema – everything from Ray to Ozu, and Tarkovsky to Rohmer (he didn't like Italian films) – and to many of the cut-price delights that London had to offer, from Japanese drummers at the university theatre (his idea) to an Indian play about Tughlaq at the Commmonwealth Institute (mine). Our conversations were companionable and jovial; intellectual, too, but rarely academic. He left to spend a fortnight in Italy at the end of August. We met again on campus at the beginning of October.

When I had finished school at eighteen, I'd failed to agree with my parents about what I should be doing at university. My tutors had recommended that I study English at Sussex, while my father wanted me to read Law at Oxford, as he had done. I hadn't found a place for either, and had been offered a History and Languages programme in a Hertfordshire college, where all I'd gained, before I dropped out after a year, was a beginner's knowledge of Spanish. Later, instead of studying, I travelled around Italy and Spain, picking up the languages in Rome and Milan, Barcelona and Murcia. Then I worked in the bank for over a year, because my parents said, when I turned twenty-one, that I should do something useful: they couldn't keep on giving me an allowance merely to pursue my hobbies. I loathed my job. I saved, then applied for a partial scholarship to fulfil my dream of studying Persian. My father agreed to cover the substantial short-fall. (He didn't approve of my choice; my mother, I thought, covertly did.)

Marco had joined university a year before me: he was studying Urdu and History, and had taken Persian as a minor in his first year. He'd wanted to leave Italy because, he said, classes there went so slowly that it was difficult to finish your studies before you were thirty. One advantage of being with Marco was that we spoke either Italian or Urdu to each other and didn't need English at all, which gave us a special kind of ease.

Our department was a temple, ruled by the formidable camel-riding personage Marco had dubbed Lady L. Lady Jane would have been a more appropriate title: she was born into the minor nobility but had never married, and would not have been addressed as Lady Lambert. In the hallowed halls of Middle Eastern Studies she was known as The Professor and reputed to be a martinet, or, at her less than benign best, an academic Mary Poppins. She was tall, thin and hollow-cheeked; she scraped back her steel-wire hair into a little bun. She wore masculine tweed jackets over severely tailored skirts. But her accent when she spoke Persian was soft, and sometimes she pinned an agate brooch above a breast. Marco said I was her *'fiore all'occhiello'*, or, as we say in Urdu, 'the star of her eye', because I managed to get my verbs right in the first weeks of term. He had not, I gathered, been very happy in her class.

There was a rumour in the corridor, carried to me as usual by Marco, that Lady L had once loved an Iranian, probably of a lower class than she was, to whom she had almost certainly and secretly been married. She had left him, chosen never to go back to Iran (or Persia, as she called it), but kept her faith with the foreign land she knew in her youth by teaching verbs, clauses and nouns to one generation after another in the language she might have learned for her lover who knew no English. And he – who knows? – he may have given her the agate, which was the kind of stone people often wore, set in rings and lockets, with prayers in Arabic letters carved into its deep orange.

It was a time when Europeans were drawn to oriental studies, and London was the centre for eastern languages. I met Riccarda Gris Santini, who was half-Italian (or half-Roman, as she said) in my

Persian grammar class. She had reddish-brown hair, cat eyes, a tigress's body, a creeping feline allure. Her voice was soft, her diction clear, her English only slightly accented. We became friends within a week: neither of us went down to the noisy, grubby cafeteria for lunch, preferring to sit in the comfortable chairs in the vestibule at the end of the corridor and eat our sandwiches there. We began talking when she offered me espresso from a flask and I thanked her in Italian. At the end of the first week, she was addressing me with the familiar 'tu'. We always sat next to each other during lessons.

Lady L occasionally attacked her for making a simple error of pronunciation or wrongly conjugating a verb, and once Riccarda sat there with tears pouring down her cheeks while the august professor ignored her distress. She and I would often study together in the evenings, at her kitchen table. Sometimes we would go together to watch Persian films with titles like *The Bicycle* or *The Cow* at a cinema in South Kensington with the curious name of Paris Pullman, which was an easy walk away from where she lived in a sprawling ground-floor flat in Barkston Gardens.

Marco called her the mystery woman; we knew she was married, because the teachers always addressed her as Mrs Santini. But it was only later and gradually that I pieced together her private life. She had been a concert pianist – a child performer in her Latin American youth, when she accompanied her Argentinian father, the renowned cellist Armando Gris, on tour; and quite successful in Europe later, until, at thirty-two, she married a Swiss banker, with whom, for years, she moved around in the Middle East and Africa. He didn't like her to play, except at parties. She had also developed stage fright, and often dreamed that she was performing in her underwear, or that she couldn't read a score and was improvising. For a while, she had lived in Iran with her husband; she developed an interest in photographing statues, monuments and old buildings there. When he was transferred to Kuwait, she'd moved to London, where, depending on the day of the week, she attended Persian classes as an external student, or studied photography with a master photographer. She had a son of fourteen, who was at boarding school in Switzerland. Though she was autonomous throughout the week, her Saturdays and Sundays were busy: I assumed that either, or both, of the males in her life could turn up or demand her presence at any time, except when she was hidden away from the world in the pied-à-terre in Rome she had inherited from her mother. The more I saw of her, the more she seemed to be caged in glamorous seclusion, like a ruler's widow: but her yearning to escape her confinement had never left her. I suppose I should say that she was forty-five when we met.

If you'd met me before I joined university and asked me then about my life, I'd have shrugged and said, 'I was born in Karachi. Grew up there. Studied in India for a couple of years. Then came to live here at sixteen.' In fact, I turned sixteen nearly a year after I arrived, just before East Pakistan split away to become Bangladesh. But my mother hadn't finally left Pakistan till the war broke out, and presenting my departure as a result of war and strife sounded more convincing as a valid reason for leaving. It was easiest to talk about my thirteen years in Karachi, say I didn't remember it well because I'd been away so long, and dismiss my time in India as two lost years in a dreary boarding school in a damp, chilly mountain town in the south, a place at least as foreign to me as Europe. My father had moved to England in the late sixties, and we had a flat overlooking the park for the first few years of my life here; then one or both of my parents took to spending more and more time (especially the colder months) in India, or Pakistan, summoned by matters of property, family ties and old loyalties. After selling the parkside flat at a loss, they had rented and then bought a smaller flat I found for them on the edge of St John's Wood. My older sister Sabah met her husband in Bombay, where she'd gone to a family wedding in 1972; he was the bridegroom's brother. Two years later, in her mid-twenties, she married and moved to Delhi. Sara, the youngest, was studying in Kent and was engaged to an Englishman she had met there. Whatever else had happened in the years between my arrival and my entry into university didn't seem to matter. I finished school, learned a few languages, travelled in Italy, France and Spain, but I drifted through all that without really caring.

So I didn't have much to say about myself, and avoided talking about my eight British years. Easy enough with Riccarda, who had so much to tell: tales of her travels, stories of books she'd read, plays she'd seen, concerts she'd performed, and the time when, in Paris, she'd played accompanist, at a tiny gathering, to the ageing, ailing Callas. (The children of estranged parents and emigrants have much in common. They learn early to elide most details, and to embroider a significant few. Riccarda was both.) Then she started asking me questions: about my childhood, school, friendships, love. When I shrunk away or mumbled, she would say: 'Talk to me. No masks please.' I would have thought of myself as awkward, yes, even timid in a way, but never masked. I found that she, too, like me, had left home young; she lived in France for some years, and then in Buenos Aires with her father and stepmother, until her father died of a heart attack and she was forced to return to her mother and Rome. 'I was seventeen. I spoke Italian with an Argentinian accent. My mother added an extra letter to my name and Ricarda Gris became Riccarda the Roman.'

Marco was excluded from our outings. Riccarda

didn't like him, found him coarse-grained, his Roman accent grating, his tastes philistine; she couldn't understand why he was doing Persian or South Asian studies. Luckily, there was no chance of his resenting our sessions at the kitchen table, where there was no room for him: he had left Lady L's basic grammar course the previous year, after just one term.

Lady L summoned me to her office one afternoon after class. Was it my moment of disgrace? My knees trembled, my shoulders quaked.

'Mr Meer,' she said, 'are you a sporting man?'

(So I'd been accused of gambling? But wait.)

'I mean, do you play cricket, football, tennis …?'

'No, Professor.'

'I was merely asking in case you wanted Wednesday afternoons off in order to play.'

(She made some reference to my being young, energetic, and in need of constant exercise. But if I could ever get away early from classes, I would rush to an office a mile's walk away to file papers for a small sum that kept me in Jacques Brel LPs, cigarettes, Italian paperbacks and cinema tickets for the month. I had taken a studio flat a mile away from my parents, so I could work alone, and had to pay the rent. Although the time off to work extra hours and earn more money would actually have helped, my studies, too, were important that first year. I wasn't going to take any chances.)

'I wouldn't want to miss a class.'

'Oh, good man. But if some day you'd like a game of squash, I play on Thursday evenings.'

I didn't play squash, and, as a consequence, perhaps, I fell from grace.

1979

It was happenstance, of course: Lady L and her old adversary Reza Shah falling in the same year, he from his throne, she from her bicycle. (Perhaps I never had lost her favour in the few months – was it even six? – I was under her tutelage. I don't remember. Life has a way of taking over from memory.) I recall the hours spent over verbs and tenses and subjunctives, and the rise of Khomeini, and the hanging of Bhutto, and the gentle middle-aged Persian native who took me over from Lady L when she went on protracted leave after an accident. (Her broken limb gave rise to a battle of succession, and she never did reclaim her role as High Priestess of Persian in the department.) Marco, who had switched from Persian to Hindi, laughed at me. 'Trust you to choose to study Persian, Mehran, just as Iran's star is falling and the stock of Arabic rises.' And Thatcher won the elections at some point. Pakistan had let me down by letting Bhutto be hanged and ogre-faced Zia take over with his henchmen. Iran, too, which seemed to offer me some sort of alternative, was now becoming a kind of dictatorship; I would not be going there for a long while yet. I drifted away from Tina, who spent more time in Venice and Milan than in London and was too absent a partner for a twenty-four year old; instead I hung around university bars with Marco and others, went to midweek socials in the evenings in the idle hope of meeting someone new; rushed between work and classes when I did more of the former and attended fewer of the latter; and often spent Saturdays alone at the cinema, a concert, or with a pile of records or a book, or writing down my thoughts and reflections for hours in my notebooks between pages of grammar exercises and passages of translation.

In the first year at university, Urdu had been, in a way, my default subject, coming second to Persian just as it had come second to English all my life. The tutors of Urdu were quiet scholarly men in their late twenties and early thirties, who revolved around another charismatic figure: Mr Dick of the curly grey locks and portly body, a Marxist who still read all literature in terms of class struggle and economic monopolies, but had a sensitive and paradoxical, though erratic, understanding of traditional Urdu poetry: like Lukacs, he probably held that a culture's decadent writers best exposed its shortcomings from the inside, while radicals and revolutionaries indulged, on the page, in wishful thinking. He held that in the century he loved best, the eighteenth, Urdu poets were still artisans, who practised their craft like jewellers or potters, working with inherited patterns and ritualised designs rather than voicing an individual agony, apart from a few honourable exceptions. But Mr Dick's reputation, in contrast to Lady L's, was confined to our corridors.

I only had to attend one seminar a week, with students who had started a year or two ahead of me, in which one student had to deconstruct an Urdu poem. There were close readings and discussions by students from the final year of Faiz or Iqbal, the moderns who had first inspired me, in my teens, to read Urdu poetry. Or we discussed classic lyrics, Wali and Quli and Sauda and Ghalib, for two hours. My Urdu spelling was atrocious, but I discovered a talent I had never suspected I had for unravelling elaborate similes and undoing the multiple knots of a metaphor. Much of the time, I just had to pick up xeroxed copies of prose texts like *Bagh-o-bahar* (*The Garden and Spring: or the Tale of Four Dervishes*) and *Umrao Jan Ada*, read them alone without supervision, and deliver a scribbled exegesis, a report, or (now and then) a few pages of translation.

I'd been disappointed to hear that Lady L wouldn't be teaching me again. Somehow the few months I had been her favourite student had given me some sense of purpose and orientation, even though her classes hadn't taken me in the literary direction I expected. By the time I began my second year, Riccarda had left and was taking photographs in Turkey and Indonesia. I was left entirely alone in the Persian class, hunching over the homilies of Sa'adi, or Qabus' advice to his son, in which all manner of conduct from letter-writing to personal hygiene was strictly codified. But I soon adjusted to the fresh rhythm of poring over texts, without companions or classmates, in the company of my new and less charismatic tutors. Persian Studies meant, for me, the subtle disciplines of word order and subjunctives and parsing, and then the vagaries of translation, which – I was often reprimanded by yet another tutor, a sandy Englishman who didn't quite seem to know what he was doing with the Persian canon – I practised too freely or too literally.

I'm sure that my training in Persian helped me to navigate the maze of my own language, but I can't remember ever studying a Persian poem, with Lady L or any of my other teachers. Rumi's *Masnavi* I read with my mother in my teens; the subtleties of Hafez I would struggle with later, on my own. Urdu was much easier than Persian. I spent my childhood in Karachi with my ear to the radio, listening to musical settings of many of the verses I was now studying, and could recite poems by heart without even realising that they were the work of classical (or modern) masters. I absorbed their vocabulary and the rules of prosody through music, and didn't even know how sound my understanding of rhythm and metre was. Then, living in India as a teenager, I learned to like Bombay movies, and for a time their sentiment and melodrama, even when it was excessive, had seemed more real to me than life. Though I didn't know Sanskrit, I recognised its rhythms too. And there was my mother, the songs I heard her sing: my musical education must have helped to develop my ear for the melody of the written sentence.

That autumn, Marco and I began our twice-weekly seminars with Mr Dick. We read long romantic poems by Mir and Shauq and Mir Hassan, Sauda's satires and Anis's laments for the martyrs of Karbala, all eloquently expressed in the most lucid language. If there was any excess at all it was not of verbiage but of emotion, which didn't disturb me: it reminded me of a more intense and somehow purified version of the sentiments in the popular songs on the radio I grew up listening to and still hummed. I didn't have to think much, or prepare much; just prise open the text so it could reveal its mysteries, or read the words out loud and let the poems talk to me, their rhythms singing in my head. Now I realised that the rolling cadences of Keats and Tennyson had always been a music as distant from my ear as the assonances of Mir or Ghalib or Faiz were close.

'The last gasp of a dying, feudal culture!' Dick intoned in his first lecture, then half-chanted a verse by Mir: '*Aag the ibtida-i-ishq men ham/ab jo hain khak intiha hai ye.*' He followed this with his own translation: 'I was all fire when first I fell in love / Now at the last nothing but ash remains.' Mir, he said, was probably the only one of the eighteenth-century poets in whose writings the melancholy fire of lived experience smouldered. Dick was also a champion of Nazir Akbaradi, an eighteenth-century schoolmaster from Agra about whom he had written a classic volume, *The Unsung Poet*, on which he had built his reputation. Nazir wrote in demotic language and unpretentious metres about normal everday events; his poems had titles like 'Hunger', 'Bread', 'Poverty' and 'The Gypsy's Song.'

> Man is fire and man is light,
> A man will guide you through the night,
> Then say goodbye, and that's the end.
> You'll never know he was your friend.

Because Nazir chafed against the constraints of Persian verse, Dick saw him as an embodiment of the common spirit. I hated his rough language and rustic imagery, and often argued about him with Marco, who lauded his use of Hindi vernacular. (In response to Nazir's verse about a cucumber, he

declaimed: *'Pane! Pane di ogni bocca!'** 'That's not
Nazir', I said. 'No, it's Pablo Neruda.The Nazir of
our time.')

Marco endeared himself to Dick, who found me
aloof and aristocratic, called me The Nawabzada
behind my back, and didn't at all understand why I
was in an Urdu class and not at Oxbridge. (He said
so to Marco, probably knowing that the story would
be retold and I would hear it. As I did.)

* 'Bread! Bread for every mouth!'

1980

In class, Marco was reading out the lines '*dekh lo aaj ham ko ji bhar ke / koi aata nahin hai phir mar ke*'* from '*Zehr-i-Ishq*'. Listening to his soft, dry voice, accompanied by the sound of the wind in the leaves outside, I could just hear the silk-wrapped arpeggios of Tahira Syed (who had recently recorded a musical arrangement of that section of the poem) echo in my head. Suddenly Dick guffawed: 'Oh, like so much nineteenth-century Urdu literature, this is at the level of Victorian penny dreadfuls.' And I, who had never even heard of Edward Said or his emerging theories, exploded: 'But that sort of comparison is facile! I don't see why you're making it.' I don't remember Dick's response: it was probably dismissive, but I had made my point.

'*Zehr-i-Ishq*' or 'The Poison of Love', one of our

* 'Look at me to your heart's content / no one returns from the dead'

set texts, was from the second half of the nineteenth century: it was the story of a youth who fell in love at first sight with the girl next door and had an affair with her in a society which secluded its women and didn't allow romance. Its heroine spent a long time dying. Why couldn't the hero, I asked myself, simply have pleaded with his parents to bring her to their home as his bride? Even in my childhood I had heard accounts of unfortunate love affairs that had ended in family reconciliations. On the other hand, there was also the story of my great-uncle Rafi, who was unlucky in love and died young (of grief, I couldn't help thinking). But the death throes of Shauq's poem gave the language one of its most stirring romantic ballads. As for our other texts, the poem '*Muamlat-i-Ishq*' ('Matters of Love'), by the hugely celebrated Mir, was also the story of a grand, tragic and adulterous love – it ended, though, in madness, not death. Our tutors, admirers of the late Mughal eighteenth century, preferred its tougher timbre to Shauq's sensuousness; they held that after the 1857 Uprising (which they still called a mutiny) nothing of merit had been written in the classical tradition and only reformist poets like Hali, with their English influences, were worth reading. I was drawn to Shauq's almost cinematic romanticism, which caused constant debates in our three-man class. Then, of course, there was Mir Hassan's perennial wonder tale in verse: '*Sihr-ul-Bayan*' ('The

Enchantment of the Tale), the story of Benazir, the Bad Fairy Mahrukh, and the Princess Badremunir. I knew it from my great-aunt's version, which as a child I often heard her tell. But I hadn't known its title, or which came first, the written tale or the pithier version my great-aunt told. And as for the Bad Fairy, I would rather not have remembered the nightmare figure of my childhood she evoked.

I had, at some uncharted stage, left behind the rhetorical delights of the *Book of Persian Grammar* and immersed myself in the intricacies of my rediscovered mother tongue. Poetry was, after all, what I had come in search of. But while Persian had taught me the discipline of grammar and translation, and Urdu the joy of lyricism, I was also acquiring new vocabularies of emotion. I don't know when it was, precisely: in one of those moments of crisis about present and future that males in their twenties sometimes experience, I had turned to Riccarda instead of Marco for advice, and I realised how close we had become even while we conjugated Persian verbs together. (Elective affinities, she held, were stronger and more important than ties of blood.)

Summer. I sat my finals in Persian, did quite well, and left it behind as an academic subject for ever. Lady L had come back by then, her hair cropped close. But she was a shadowy figure among the library shelves.

I don't think she recognised me when I greeted her. I soon stopped acknowledging her, except with the vaguest of nods.

I posed for Riccarda's camera in the park during the summer vacation. The photographs she took of me – on the riverbank, looking at the river, feeding ducks in the park, reading Kalidasa's *Meghaduta* in Italian, staring at a tree, embracing it, smiling, solemn – show a youth more rough and rugged than I imagined myself to be. 'How happy we look,' she remarked about a photograph of us against the sunlit backdrop of the Serpentine. (We had been eating ice cream there between photographs and run into a PhD student who had taught us basic Arabic broken plurals in Lady L's absence; he had taken the photograph with Riccarda's camera, and captured something neither of us was aware of.)

The most considerate of friends when she chose to be, Riccarda was also, at times, curiously absent-minded and elusive. 'Sagittarians can be uncaring! My moon is in Aquarius too. A terrible moon for a woman.' And all too often, when her wanderlust took her away in search of foreign scenes to capture with her camera's eye, she just wasn't there.

I hadn't wanted to make friends in Urdu or History: I no longer had much in common with my friends from other places. But I always seemed to be helping Marco, with vocabulary, syntax and pronunciation. In those autumn days, crisp and cool and rosy like apples, it was Marco's presence that filled my narrow room; his surprisingly deep voice intoning planned trajectories, dreams, activities, always navigating the future, while my map was scaled very small.

'No one loves me for myself,' he lamented one afternoon. 'Only for my body. I've always known I was seductive.'

I looked at him in wonder, not knowing whether he was joking or not. Just once I met the girl he often talked about, Caroline, the object of whose occasionally unwanted affections he was. Blonde, tall and strong, a countrywoman to the tips of her sensible shoes, she looked as if she could carry him around a farm on her shoulders. 'I've always been too busy with girls to have much time for friendship,' he told me: I didn't ask him whether the many hours he claimed of my time were his way of compensating for a lack of friendship in his life. Occasionally, as we talked or listened to records, he would fall asleep with his head against the wall and I'd pull him, grunting, down to my carpeted floor, cover him with a quilt or a sheet and let him sleep on till it was time for him to rise, make coffee and heat up whatever he could find – pasta, lentils, rice, meat – then shower (or not) before leaving for classes.

I had acquaintances with whom I'd drink coffee, and other warmer friends to dine at home with once in a while. But it was years since I'd been very close to anyone, male or female. I'd had a few girlfriends. But the first one – the only one with whom I really fell in love – hurt me when I was seventeen (she went off to America before my birthday, and never even sent a card). After that I was quite casual in my physical relationships. I never made the first move, usually only responding to women who showed an interest in me. Sex had always been an ambivalent need, either a passing physical craving or, more often, hunger for reassurance.

Because I travelled so much as a child and adolescent, I was used to leaving friendships behind. When I came to London, I thought nothing of spending a day or two in intense conversation with someone I might never see again: time shared was no guarantee of lasting friendship. But there were people who found my manner disconcerting: expected my deep and continuing friendship, when really all I'd done was have a conversation with them in a cafeteria or in a park. I wanted to travel light: too much affection was burdensome, it led to dependency, and with my solitary habits I couldn't deal with that, not in myself, not in others.

Now I suddenly had two intimate and sometimes competing friendships. But Riccarda – who now sometimes called on weekends – could be elusive, and Marco, for all his claims on my time, was too spiky and proud to put himself in a position where I might rebuff him. Except when it came to Riccarda.

'You drop me when she beckons,' he complained when I told him I couldn't see him on a Friday evening because she'd invited me to a family dinner. 'She's too old for you, you know.'

'Don't talk rubbish.'

'Well, you know what people think; everyone gossips about the two of you. By the way, what happened to Tina? Did she dump you? I saw her with an older guy at the cinema. He looked rich. She said I should call her, though.'

But with Riccarda I allowed myself reactions I rarely had before. If I didn't hear from her for a week, I would miss her. When once she left me standing at her door for an hour in the rain and explained she had been busy shopping for porcelain with visiting friends, I retorted: 'If you're always so caught up with foreign visitors, what's the point of making appointments with me, or having friends in London? We might as well be living in different cities.'

She was startled: I had never spoken so sharply to her.

At times I felt guilty for constantly keeping Marco on standby, though his own offhand manner was a great protection. If I cancelled a meeting, he too had to study, and wouldn't have made it; if I rang him on the off-chance, something he had planned had just fallen through and he was free. Once I found myself with a spare ticket I had saved for weeks to buy, for a Juliette Greco concert, for Riccarda: she had said, at the last minute, she couldn't come. I hadn't seen Marco that day, and I left a note in his pigeonhole saying I'd wait at the Embankment till 6.40 pm, a little before the concert began at the Queen Elizabeth Hall. He was waiting on the embankment when I got there. 'Just so you wouldn't have to sit through it alone.' I didn't, though he offered, take the money for the ticket from him.

A couple of times, if he didn't pick up the phone when I had promised to call and was late, I was vaguely disappointed. But he spent at least one weekday and almost every Friday evening at my house, and some Sunday afternoons at the cinema with me; I felt it was only fair that he should have some other interests apart from his classes at university, the swimming pool at the students' union, and the fortnightly weekends he spent in Berkshire with Caroline's family.

I tried several times to take Marco and Riccarda out together, to films and concerts or even just to a pub. One night at my kitchen table before we went to see a late-night show of *Company Limited*, they argued, as if by agreement, about everything – the pronunciation of the word 'costolette', the architectural merit of the Hayward Gallery, the films of the Tavianis or Wajda. Later, Marco found an excuse to turn on me and say: 'You're so Anglicised, all your knowledge of Urdu poetry comes from listening to recordings of *ghazals* by pop stars and pretty female singers – it's the music and the easy lyricism you love, not the underlying philosophy.' I didn't respond.

There was a side of Riccarda I glimpsed on rare occasions, when we went dancing with friends. (She, at forty-seven, the oldest of us.) She drank deep and danced wild till dawn, intoxicated more by her own longings than any alcohol she'd had: longings for a past she'd lost, or a future she knew did not await her. She danced like a slave in a field, re-enacting some half-forgotten ritual, limbs twisting, hands on breasts or hip or groin, shocking hapless younger partners.

One of these partners was Marco, who took us one evening to a club on Bond Street where couples of the same sex could dance together. After a few drinks, she decided to dance with us both. But it was Marco she was challenging. Like a tiger, circling a fine thoroughbred pony. He met the challenge well – he was graceful on the dance floor. I left them, feeling vaguely excluded, and sat down by the wall with a glass of iced whisky to watch them. They were on the floor for an hour. Riccarda finally seemed to snap out of her trance, and they walked towards me. Marco was smiling. He grabbed my glass and drank it down in one gulp. 'Hot,' he muttered, and though it was a late November night, I saw that his face was shining with sweat, his shirt was open to his belt, and his grey suit was clinging to his body. Riccarda, on the contrary, in her blue jeans and baggy striped shirt, looked as if she'd just stepped out of a beauty salon.

Later, as Riccarda was driving us back, she said: 'I don't quite know how to get to Bloomsbury, Marco. I'll drop you both off at Mehran's.' Mmm, Marco grunted. In fact, she dropped us off a block away from where I lived, and Marco, rather than stopping for the night bus, followed me home. I went to bed almost as soon as we got home – I didn't have a head for spirits, had knocked back a couple of whiskys at the nightclub, and must have fallen asleep while he was washing. I woke in the middle of the night from a deep sleep to feel something weighing on my heart, only to find it was Marco's hand. He was recumbent next to me, in his shirt and his grey suit trousers and shoes still on, on my narrow bed, snoring softly, his head on my shoulder. I didn't move, thinking of the double vodkas Riccarda had plied him with, but at some point, half-asleep, I watched him rise, stretch, look around him, pick up his jacket from the floor, strip down to his vest and briefs and lie down by the wall where I had left his usual quilt for him before I went to bed.

In December – a fortnight after that encounter –
Marco left London for the Christmas holidays. He
didn't return. There was a complicated administra-
tive reason. He was registered at the University of
Rome (or Naples, I never quite understood). It was
there that he would have to write and submit his
dissertation. He hadn't explained any of this to me
when he left. He just rang up from Frascati on New
Year's Day; asked me to redeem his collection of
matchboxes from his hostel near Brunswick Square,
and to get a refund for his library ticket, which he
had also left in his room. It didn't occur to me that
he had intended to be back; I only thought he'd been
furtive about his plans, or at best careless, and he
hadn't said goodbye.

1981

One last term: the final months of my undergraduate degree. I had a handful of stories from the twenties, thirties and forties, by Premchand and Manto, to read, shrill pieces of polemic that didn't appeal to me. There were poems by Iqbal, which I admired, and by Faiz, whose work I had always loved above all other poets' since I discovered, at sixteen, a bilingual volume of his poems on a shelf of the modern languages section at my local library. But Dominic, the young man who taught me modern Urdu poetry and probably understood it about as well as I did, said: 'Everything Iqbal wrote was derived from Nietzche and Bergson; Faiz habitually plagiarises Yeats and even Tennyson.' He seemed unaware that they were master craftsmen in a grand tradition directly influenced by Rumi and Hafiz.

For an hour a week I also studied Sindhi and Siraiki poetry with Dominic, the one tutor in our department who knew the languages and loved vernacular poetry. Since I didn't have time to learn the harsh, graceful languages my father had spoken as a boy and then lost, I would study a page or two from a grammar book and then attempt to decipher the texts of the poems with vocabularies. What I really wanted was to understand the work of Shah Abdul Latif, Sachal Sarmast and Kwaja Ghulam Farid, the great poets of the Indus Valley who used those age-old tales of blighted loves my mother had told us to map the experiences of the soul's longing for its origins. I would finally only have to write an essay on the use of folktales in mystic poetry with the help of translations; but my love for music meant that I could spend hours listening to recordings of the finest musicians singing these poems, their voices ripping into me with the sharpness of one of the daggers which in their songs they often plunged into their own breasts or those of other hapless lovers.

Much of the time I worked alone on my dissertation on realism and romance in three *masnavi*s. (I was working on the rise of romantic individualism in Urdu poetry, and poets who, by using a confessional 'I', had closed the gap between artist and artisan. I had argued to include Shauq: Dick would have preferred an essay on the elegant eighteenth century, his own favourite era, but I cleverly said I would talk about the decadent aesthetic of the later poet.) At least in this obscure corner I escaped the shadow of English literature and French and German philosophy.

University hadn't been the haven I imagined, or not for long; much of what I learnt about the poetry I was looking at I acquired on my own. But it had provided me with texts and contexts, kept me safe in the closed circle of my studies and given me an introduction to Riccarda. And I had an idea now of where to go. My tutors had my apprenticeship planned. A PhD in the unexplored literary genre of the nineteenth-century Muharram elegy. And then, perhaps, tenure. I thought I was protected for the next three years. Yet in the darkening winter days, during Riccarda's longer absences, I no longer had the consolation of Marco's company.

But whenever Riccarda was in town I discovered a city I had hardly charted, hidden within the London I thought I knew well. My first taste of sushi in a wooden bar in Covent Garden. Sian Phillips singing 'Bewitched, Bothered and Bewildered' in the West End revival of *Pal Joey*. Pasolini's *Medea* at the art house cinema in Brunswick Square. The Impressionists at the Tate, the Contemporary Dance Theatre at The Place in Euston. And I took her to hear Leonard Cohen sing, and see a new Pakistani film, *The Blood of Hussein,* which combined the poetry of Shia mourning rituals with protest against a dictatorial regime.

Riccarda's habitat, I knew by now, was an elegantly constructed paper house: her relationships with her husband and son were of paper too, exquisitely patterned but fragile. I wouldn't ever have asked, but her behaviour at the club confirmed what I had already guessed. (She also told me, in a reversal of our former roles of confessor and confidant, that she'd stopped seeing her photographer, who had been both her mentor and her lover: she said she probably only imagined that he ever loved her.)

In April, she took me out to celebrate my twenty-sixth birthday at Mr Chow's in Knightsbridge. (*O cuore! Congedati, e vivi!** she wrote on the flyleaf of the copy of Pavese's diaries, *The Business of Living,* she gave me as a present.) I told her over candles and champagne that I had loved her for a long time without even knowing that I did.

I have a photograph of that evening. She's dressed in a blue outfit she bought in India, a long, clinging shirt over narrow trousers. Her blue eyes smile at the camera. I'm dressed in white; I'm grinning into my glass.

The rest takes place off the page.

* 'Oh heart! Be free, and live!'

I sat my finals in the middle of the year. Marco and I had started writing each other long, occasional letters a few months after he left, and our exchanges had become lively again. To celebrate what he called the end of my captivity, he invited me to spend a fortnight with him in Italy. When he came to meet me at the airport, he seemed looser, happier, in his own place. We spent time in Frascati, and travelled together to his parents' farm in the countryside near Lake Bracciano. One day he came upon me lazily writing Riccarda's name in the dust in Persian letters; I quickly erased the signs, but I think he knew what I was doing. Then Riccarda called to say that she was waiting for me in Rome: her cousin was exhibiting her sculptures and I could say I was attending the opening. Marco's response to hearing I was going to leave him early was to offer to drive me to Rome. He didn't seem to realise, at first, that I was leaving him, but when he did he said in a tone that was wry but indulgent: 'One message from Madame X and you're dumping me. I guess I should be jealous. Never mind, lots of beauties around.'

He dove, brown and bare-skinned, into the lake. I hadn't told him, but he had guessed when she called, that I was going to spend a few well-planned days with Riccarda in Rome. The next morning he took me in a borrowed car to the station twenty miles away, held me close to his chest when we parted, and made me promise to meet him in India in winter.

Rome, in August, was drowsy, apricot-gold; sultrily abandoned to its silver fountains and its deep blue skies. For the first time in years, I began to imagine what it might be like to live away from London, the city that had been my only home for eleven years. Riccarda and I stayed together in Trastevere, at the apartment of Riccarda's blonde and vibrant cousin Lilla, a sculptor and a poet, the opening of whose exhibition I had ostensibly come to Rome to attend.

Lilla knew when to leave us alone. Evenings the three of us would often spend together, sometimes in the company of friends, where I was introduced as Riccarda's erstwhile desk-mate or as Lilla's intellectual friend. Lilla would cook risotto with artichokes, or spaghetti with scallops and shrimps. Roman nights were lush; it even rained a few times. We would walk arm in arm, the three of us, singing Roman and Neapolitan songs; I remember Riccarda well, wandering around the streets of Rome in cotton trousers, her hair windblown, her lips and skin unpainted.

And the afternoons Riccarda and I spent in a darkened room, on a low white bed nearly as big as the room it was in, playing, naked, for hours. Free with each other as we had never been before, like children. Tickling and nipping, wrestling, laughing, splashing white wine on each other's skin and kissing it off. I had never known that kind of freedom, never been so aware of my body being so full of pleasurable places. Riccarda's body was golden all over, and almost perfect; but she thought her firm breasts were too small for her hips. She had a slim waist and resembled a figurine when she was naked. 'When you're dressed,' I told Riccarda, 'you look like a queen. When you're naked you are a goddess.'

Then the call came that broke our enchantment. Her son and her husband were arriving unexpectedly in Rome that evening. She had to leave Lilla's place right away. I don't know how they found out or what she had told them she was doing in Rome. Oh, yes, she was attending Lilla's exhibition, that was true; she'd done the photographs for the catalogue. I knew Riccarda had to leave soon, to join her husband and son in Tunisia, but they weren't meant to be in Rome: we were supposed to have had three more days together. I had a fixed booking on a flight back to London that I couldn't change. I would have to buy another ticket.

I didn't say much. What could I say?

Riccarda must have seen my euphoria turn to misery. She suggested I stay on with Lilla in Rome, but Lilla, too, was preparing to leave for Venice.

'Where's your friend … Marco?' Riccarda asked. 'Can't you join him for a few days?'

I shook my head.

'He has his own plans. I'm going back. No point in staying on without you.'

She offered me money, to travel in Italy, or for a ticket home. I didn't take it.

'It all happened so fast,' she said when we parted. 'I'm confused.'

I wished I could talk to Marco, confide in him. Have one or two days more with him by the lake. Or tell him to come back to Rome: he might, on his motorbike. But I didn't call him. I couldn't bear to tell him what had happened, it would be like putting myself at his mercy. Instead I spent a day in Rome alone with Lilla. I couldn't change my booking; I couldn't find another cheap flight, and I couldn't afford a full fare.

Lilla drove me to the station to take a train back to London. 'Typical of her,' she said. Somehow I knew it wasn't the first time she'd been left to look after one of Riccarda's lovers.

It took me thirty-six hours or more to get back to London; I travelled via Milan, changed stations at Paris, took the ferry at Calais. I cried on the boat and pretended I had hay fever in the sunny August weather. After Riccarda's sudden flight I knew that our relationship would always be full of interruptions and breaks. I had always wanted to hold on to her, missed her while she was away and found her elusive, so I gambled my body for her love, thinking that once we were lovers I would have a bigger place in her heart. I had failed. Looking at the whitish waters of the Channel now, I was making other plans: dreaming, for the first time since 1979, the year I dreamed of going off to Shiraz or Isfahan to study Persian literature there once I had learned enough grammar from Lady L. Now, again, I wanted to travel, to write essays or poems, or a short film script, perhaps, to live for a while in another country. I thought I should write a doctoral thesis or at least go along with my tutor's suggestion that I write one. Then I would settle down with someone and have a child, or adopt one, while I was still young. No room in my life for a secretive lover. I took the train from Dover to Victoria, and reached home dirty and dishevelled.

Riccarda came back to London in early October. We met in the lobby of the Hilton in Holland Park and were sipping coffee in the open-plan bar. Riccarda had ordered a cognac to go with her espresso. It was two in the afternoon. She was, again, the Riccarda I'd first met: perfectly groomed in her lightweight, dark-blue jacket and knee-baring skirt, her shoulder-length hair, unusually, pulled away from her face.

My father had given me an open ticket to India

as a graduation present. I hadn't been able to go back to India with my mother when my grandmother died, as I was in the middle of my exams, but the time, he said, seemed right, while I was in a transitional phase.

'I'm going to India soon,' I told Riccarda. And she, who was always weighing her wings to fly, seemed not to understand.

'You'll be meeting that vulgar Roman boy again, I suppose. Sounds like one of his plans. Shouldn't you be looking for a job rather than exploring your roots?'

She could have been talking to her sulky adolescent son.

'Like what?' I asked. 'The FAO?' (I had just been refused a grant for postgraduate work because I hadn't done as well as I should in my History exams, and my research proposal wasn't quite interesting enough to my university for them to take a risk on me. When I told my parents, my father, absentminded as usual, had said, from behind the shelter of *The Times*: 'Well, you could always join the Food and Agriculture Organisation in Rome. With your Italian. I could always call my old friend Zaid, he'll get you an interview.')

Riccarda looked hurt. In fact, she said, she'd spoken to a film producer who might have some part-time work for me. It was the kind of work – reading and editing scripts – I wanted to do for a while. But I had yet to hear from him. Jobs of the kind I wanted were not easily available for a twenty-six year old with a degree in oriental languages.

Riccarda's son was seventeen now. She was emotionally separated from her husband, but for their son's sake they were still a couple on skiing holidays at Christmas and summers in Tunisia or Lamu. And I felt that she was giving me a message: that to expect more from her than short, intense interludes of make-believe domesticity, or secret meetings from a bad old French film, followed by absences and distances, was foolish. That courteous formality that must always have been there between us in company became more and more evident to me each time we met in public, even when we were on our own. The only place where we still made sense to each other was behind the locked door of a bedroom.

My parents, too, had begun to show concern about my unconventional 'relationship'. All the years Riccarda and I had been friends, with their tacit approval, seemed to have been forgotten.

'Even close friendships have their span,' my mother said at one of her Sunday breakfasts, looking into her gold-rimmed white teacup. (Her developing philosophy, based on one of her Persian adages, was that all relationships of love and beauty were best enjoyed from a slight distance.)

'Just don't let anyone hold you back,' my father added, spooning more scrambled eggs onto his plate. 'You need time to think. To plan your life.'

These gentle, vulnerable people, who had lived their lives according to a code of *noblesse oblige* and a set of impossibly high ideals, were trying to protect me from, and prepare me for, a world that had continued to baffle and hurt them. I knew that the trip to India was their way of separating me from her. Kindly. I was grateful to them for the reprieve.

Memory is a bad storyteller: it erases all the real twists in a tale. But when I look back it seems that all the narrative time allotted to Riccarda and me was nine days in August. Five – or was it four? – days of passion, of herself and those Roman hours, had been her spontaneous gift to me. After that her love became something she granted me, or loaned me, because I was importunate. Even when I remembered the days we had spent together, I could sense in early autumn what I hadn't wanted to see in late summer: she had counted those days, day by day, and then she had counted each hour, as you might count out the notes for a loan of cash. That the loan might be one she was making to herself I did not stop to consider. All I felt was the burden of a gift too expensive to reciprocate. Or worse, the weight in my shirt pocket, chafing my breast, of a loan of notes and coins that couldn't be repaid, only returned without interest.

We met, several times, often in public places, over the next few weeks. One night, after a showing of *La Femme du Boulanger* at the NFT, I refused to take her home when she said I should. In that no-man's tract between summer and autumn, we walked up and down on a bridge over the Thames. I can see us clearly. She's wearing a belted cream raincoat, like a man's, and a beret; I'm in blue, sleeves rolled up to the elbows, a purple sweater slung over my shoulders. But I can't hear what I say: just a few cracked and headless sentences, about needing freedom, space to find my direction. And then I fall silent.

'Talk to me, tell me,' she says.

I respond: 'But I thought I had.'

Let's not meet till you come back from India.

I think it's she who says that.

And I who want to say it.

A narrative of love, Riccarda's and mine, that is fated to remain unfinished. I won't attempt to give it closure here.

I arrived in Delhi on a November night. I had never been there before. I spent an hour in the queue before meeting Sabah and her husband Farhan, who had come to pick me up at the airport, at nearly three in the morning. On the drive home the air was heavy, foggy. The outskirts of the city were like countryside, and even in the darkness I could see the familiar dusty spaces and low-growing trees beneath which little groups of men with scarves tied around their heads sat around fires. We drove down a great avenue into the city. Tall silhouettes loomed at me from the darkness. Here and there, a fugitive lamp illuminated a reddish dome.

I was staying with Sabah and Farhan in their roomy white flat in Nizamuddin, overlooking an elegant mausoleum. The first few days were a round of visits to relatives, friends, gardens, monuments, shrines. Marco had given me the number of an old acquaintance at Jamia Millia, who, he said, would always know where he was. When I rang, a woman's irate voice told me that she didn't know where Mr Feliciani was, or even who he was. As always, I felt I had let Marco down by arriving later than he expected, and he had gone off on his travels to places he'd wanted me to see with him.

I liked Delhi, and felt I had been there before. Yet I hadn't, and it was so new: of the cities I had been to, only Rome was as densely paved with history's stones. My father had studied here in the forties; a decade or more before, mother's uncle Rafi, the writer in the family, had often stayed in Daryaganj, in the old part of town, and fallen in love with the daughter of distant cousins who lived in the neighbourhood. Farhan took me to bookshops in Old Delhi, where on the pavements I found more books about the subjects I was meant to research than I would ever read, but Rafi's book of stories wasn't available and no one had heard of it.

But I discovered more about the writer and his work, from Annie, my mother's friend, herself a lauded and much-loved novelist; she knew his name and his fiction, had heard stories, from her novelist parents, of his personal charm and elegance. He was known, she said, as Rafi Rangeela – Colourful Rafi. She showed me one of his stories, in an anthology of stories culled from the once popular journal called *Sarosh* to which her parents and she had often contributed. The entire story spun around a Persian proverb – 'You ought to kill a cat on the first day' – and Annie described it as a deft contemporary reworking of *The Taming of the Shrew*. It was far from exotic (as I had thought it might be); a witty satire on the emancipation of women, but not very kind to their goals.

I felt it was sentimental to talk about familiar smells and tastes and colours but I was overwhelmed by the familiarity of what I had missed for more than ten years. The particular lemon light of a November morning. The particular green of North Indian grass, the gnarled trunks of certain trees, and the flash of green parrot wings in gardens. The particular smell of peanuts roasting, sold encased in newspaper cones. The familiar sound of voices, syllables, consonants. Every time I missed Riccarda, or thought too much about her, I had something or someone to claim my attention. But then I would remember her again, her smell and the feel of her skin against mine, especially at night, and wake up from my sleep with a pounding heart and sore eyes, wondering what I'd done and how I'd had the courage to sever what we had.

I laid no claim to Delhi. And it laid only passing claim to me. I came from a seaside city, and here, though the city was beautiful in parts, the river was shallow, sluggish and unimposing. People on the streets took me for a foreigner and showed surprise when I didn't act foreign, ate with my fingers, didn't worry much about drinking the water, and spontaneously spoke what they called Hindi. But even on my first trip I wanted to know what it might be like to live there, work there. Because it wasn't mine, I could make my own place there.

'But why would you want to work here for a pittance? 10,000 rupees a month,' Farhan said 'That's the least you'll need, to survive on. No one will want to know you otherwise. Better to come here on one of your foreign grants if you want to work in peace.'

On a brisk, sunny morning about ten days after I arrived I was walking down Janpath with Farhan when we saw a European couple walking towards us. 'Hippies,' my brother-in-law muttered. The woman was small and red-haired, dressed in cheap Indian clothes; the man, in white, was draped in a black shawl, curls straggling over his shoulders from under a woollen cap.

Then the man stepped forward, arms outstretched, and flung them round my neck.

'Mehran. You finally made it.'

I placed one hand in the small of his back. He was as skinny as a goat and his smell was goat-like too.

Farhan suggested that we walk over to Nirula's coffee bar nearby, but before we reached there he remembered a lunch appointment. 'You're expected too, but I'll make your excuses,' he said. 'Shall I send the car to pick you up – in about an hour, let's say? And Marco, you must visit us. Come to dinner.'

I told him I would find my own way back and sat down to lunch with Marco and his friend. He introduced her as Paola from Naples, who was here to study Indian dance. They were living together in what, from their description, sounded like a squat. They had to share a bathroom with seven others, and much of the time there wasn't running water – they took turns to wash themselves from a bucket under a tap. They weren't very happy. The man who had promised to host Marco had let him down and he'd had his camera and his wallet stolen at a hostel he'd been at before he met Paola, and I guessed that he was very short, if not completely out, of money until his Roman family wired him some. I bought them lunch and arranged to see them at a concert the next evening.

Marco turned up alone.

Over the next few days he took me to places and showed me things I wouldn't have seen without him: art exhibitions, restaurants where you could eat traditional Muslim food, Kathak dance performances, concerts by renowned Indian classical singers. Paola, he said, had left for Lucknow. Sabah was exasperated because she kept having to make excuses to our relatives for my absences, but I reminded her I was supposed to be on a research trip and she relented: if I lunched with Marco I would have to dine with them, and if I chose to see my European friends in the daytime, I had to spend the evenings with Indian relatives and friends. I knew how tiring it was to play shepherd to someone who was a stranger to the city and virtually a tourist: she had a son not quite a year old, and must also have been relieved: she realised that someone like her brother hadn't travelled all that distance to an unknown city only to meet forgotten relatives or cousins he hadn't seen in years, much as he seemed to enjoy all that. 'Marco can come over whenever he likes,' Sabah said, but when he did visit he came up the back stairs and had a long shower in my bathroom before meeting my family. No backpack and no Indian clothes, I had told him. He'd had his hair cut short by a wayside barber and slicked it down with water. In a grey shirt of mine he looked eminently presentable. But he'd carried one of those gaudy shoulder bags of rough material that foreigners loved and left it on the floor of the sitting room. Farhan entered, said, 'What on earth is *this*?' and kicked it to one side of the room. Marco waited till he'd left the room to retrieve it.

There was no one left to visit in Indore; my uncle was teaching at Aligarh University now. But I had always planned to go to back to Agra after an absence of eleven years; Marco was always going to be my travelling companion. Farhan said he would lend me a car and Marco found a young man from Haryana who promised to drive us there. He didn't know the roads but Marco was a competent navigator and even drove much of the way. We reached Agra in the afternoon and drove straight to the Taj.

Marco was back in his hippy garb; Indian clothes in which, with his shorn head, he looked like a junkie or a mystic. He didn't like my hiring a guide; said he was always struck by how asymmetrical the architecture was, how clumsily it had tried to synthesise

Indian and Persian styles. He said he didn't like monuments to vanity. Agra was, after all, the city of Nazir, the iconoclast who'd sung: '*Sab that para reh jayega / jab lad chalega banjara*' (all splendour will lie in ruins / when the gypsy travels on). I was silent, remembering the times I was there before, with my mother and sisters and uncles; how the planes and curves and textures of the building had brought me closer than I had ever been to enchantment. And now, to an adult who had lived away from his homeland for a decade, a third or fourth sight of the edifice was even more moving than it had been to an adolescent out on a picnic with his family.

I went to wash and say a prayer in the mosque beside the Taj alone while Marco took pictures of the Yamuna River flowing behind the monument. When I came out the sun was setting and a pale gold half-moon rose. The guide, who had grown up in the neighbourhood, told us to sit on a low wall beneath the gate and just watch the colours of the stone change in the pause between twilight and the rising of the moon. Marco gasped. 'Pink, then grey, then silver, then pink again,' he murmured.

We were staying at a guest house on the outskirts of the city, and, knowing the very basic food there wouldn't suit Marco's appetite, I offered to take him to eat at a hotel in town. We showered and dressed up – I lent him a shirt – and set off. Over the very rich, creamy food and two large Indian beers he ordered, he asked me if I would travel on with him.

'I want to show you Benares,' he said. 'Allahabad. Then we'll go on to Lucknow.'

I was planning to visit Ajmer with Sabah, see my uncle in Aligarh and then fly to Bombay, from where I would go back to London. I had bought my ticket on a special deal that allowed me to stay in India a month, but if I postponed my departure I'd have to pay a forfeit. Farhan had changed my bookings soon after I arrived to allow me to leave from Bombay, as he said that travelling back to Delhi only to fly out to London again would be an unnecessary waste of a day in airports and planes.

I had only about nine days of my holiday left.

'I can't, Marco. I have to go back.'

'Mehran, we made some plans. You promised me three weeks in India. I'm sorry we couldn't meet earlier, I told you. But you said you were coming in October. When I left Rome you hadn't even booked your flight. I should have known. The bad fairy's waiting.'

For a moment I didn't know who he was talking about. Then I realised that in the last week he hadn't asked me any questions about Riccarda. And I, of course, hadn't told him that our moment, Riccarda's and mine, was over. I wanted to say something but felt it was disloyal to Riccarda.

We got back to our shared room in the guest

house. He took a shower before me and went straight to his bed. When I came out from the bathroom later his face was turned to the wall, and he didn't talk. We've been up since five, I thought: he must be exhausted. I was.

In the middle of the night I heard footsteps on the veranda. I sensed he was smoking out there. I didn't open my eyes.

Over breakfast the next day, I offered him to give him some money – what I could afford, enough to get him through a few more weeks in Delhi. He accepted, but perhaps he took offence because the day before he had criticised me for paying a guide as much as he, Marco, would spend on several meals. But that, I said, was the tariff. He argued over our differing attitudes to western tourists, whom he thought I patronised, and to privilege and entitlement. ('Since you've got here,' he said, 'you behave like one of the Indian rich.') At Itimad-ud-daula's tomb, which we visited in the morning, he was annoyed when the sight of wild dogs rolling on the graves upset me so badly that I scolded the guide and the guard for allowing them to desecrate the silence of a resting place. He said I was behaving like a bigot and a feudal. There was more: I've forgotten exactly what. Oh, yes, my wanting to visit the shrine at Fatehpur Sikri before we went to the palaces: he thought my superstitious behaviour was out of character. I just remember anger (his), coldness (mine), hurt. And though I soon forgot his words, I remember the day and the places: walking through the abandoned courtyards of Fatehpur Sikri at sunset, in the mist, and the guards telling us to leave because it was closing time, and the long, silent trip back to Delhi in the car that I had borrowed from my brother-in-law, and Marco driving all the way to Delhi with me in the back seat, and saying a quick goodbye somewhere near Connaught Place when he got out of the car and the driver took his place at the wheel.

I cancelled plans to travel to the shrine at Ajmer with my sister and left to spend the rest of my trip with family in Aligarh and Bombay.

I came back to London in mid-December. The city was dark and cold. I had given up my studio in Maida Vale before I left, and moved into my parents' flat now, because I didn't want to be alone.

Two days after I arrived, I dialled Riccarda's number, only to be greeted by the politely anonymous voice of her answering service: 'Sorry, Mrs Santini's away until the New Year. We're not at liberty to say where, but rest assured she'll get your message.'

Then snow came down and covered the pavements: we were in a white world, in the bright light of another season. Hopping off a bus, I slipped on the hard ice one evening and hurt my leg and hip badly enough to stay at home over the Christmas break, watching the kind of films I never normally would.

On the 28th, Riccarda called from Rome. She must have got my message. *Guys and Dolls* was on at the National on New Year's Day, she'd be back that morning, should she buy tickets?

Yes, I said. I was still sore and limping, and used my father's tall umbrella as a walking stick.

We met at the bar, embraced and drank the champagne she had already ordered. After the performance she took me to a wine bar where a woman in frayed jeans, who looked like an Ethiopian princess, played an electric guitar and sang jazz and blues standards. Riccarda didn't ask when I'd got back, or say anything about the two months we had been apart.

I looked at her red-brown hair, cut very short in the back now, her cat eyes and sculpted cheekbones. And I remembered everything, the smell and taste and feel of her. Instead of saying I missed her all the time I was away, and even more in the city where we both lived, I babbled on about India, but not about my longing to stay on there, to go back. Somehow I felt it would be a betrayal to talk about any of that. I talked about how, when we had been driving towards Fatehpur Sikri, I was seized with nostalgia when I saw the fields, and how I made the driver laugh when I was sentimental at the sight of piled up cakes of cow dung fuel. And I said nothing, nothing at all, about Marco being there in the back of the car.

On the bridge, light-headed with the champagne and the Chablis I had been drinking, I bent over to kiss her lips. She gave me her cheek, which was cold, and wet.

I asked if I should take her home.

'I'm not going to ask you in if you do,' she said. She was laughing.

We said goodbye at the Embankment tube station. I stopped a taxi for her, and walked to Trafalgar Square to take the night bus home.

1982

Riccarda had settled in this city, with expectations, four years ago. Now her son was going to finish school in summer, and wanted to attend university in Rome, his native place. Where once she hated to leave London for more than a few weeks, now she couldn't wait to get away. I knew her well enough to know she was planning to move back to Italy, and there was nothing I could do or say to stop her.

At times, the only enticing voices I heard echoed the siren call of the corporate world. But even if I had wanted to find my way back to the world of finance, how could I? Hadn't I done everything to escape it, more than three long years ago? In the February mornings I filled in job applications, and in the afternoons I walked to the public library and brought home volumes of plays to read, by Ibsen or Chekhov, Eugene O'Neill or Tennessee Williams. I stayed in my room and listened to flamenco or jazz or *ghazals* on my record player. Or I would spend hours writing in my notebook, reflections on life and art, worth very little to anyone but myself. I had always found it hard to shape my thoughts to write a coherent essay or an article, and only wrote spontaneously under the pressure of a test or an exam, but when I sat down with my journal I could write for hours, poems and dreams and recollections. It wasn't that I liked the act, or the activity, of writing; I just wanted to stay with my thoughts and see what I could disentangle. Even more so now, after returning from India with nothing significant to come back to.

And then the winter was gone.

After Riccarda left London in late March, I knew I had to get out of the house, further away than the library. I was jobless and dejected, had no one I could really call a friend, and my old mentors had ceased to show interest in me after I failed in my attempt to find funding for postgraduate research. Mr Dick, who called me The Nawabzada, had always found me arrogant, and hadn't endorsed any of my admittedly feeble attempts to enter the hallowed shrine of academe. My mother would tell me that I had to do something, anything, just to get away from Ibsen, Chekhov and the apartment.

My university had started to seem like one of those enchanted prisons I had read about in the romances I studied for my degree. In my dissertation – 'The Eye and the I: Realism, Romance and Magic in Three

Urdu Masnavis' – I had opted for realism, the social protest, as I saw it, of Shauq and Mir, against the romantic fantasy of 'The Enchantment of the Tale'. But what *was* real? Had the life I had lived as an undergraduate, circumscribed by my time at the university, been the model of realism I had taken it to be, or a kind of enchantment? I reminded myself of one of those heroes emerging from a short spell spent in a fairy's castle, or the rebellious and idealistic scholars who retreated from the evils of existence to a cave, to come back one day to find that a hundred years had gone by, and the world had changed so much it was no longer the place they had left behind.

I was twenty-seven, and the only work I could find was interpreting, or subtitling films and documentaries, paid by the hour, or occasional stints reading scripts or subtitling documentaries for Riccarda's friend. Sometimes I wasn't paid for months.

Then one day one of my mother's suburban protégées asked if she knew someone who could take over as a language instructor in September, to replace a colleague who had rushed off to Pakistan to take care of a sick mother. Two evening classes a week: Mondays in Holborn, Thursdays in Hendon.

'I'll do it,' I said.

In October, Marco rang me – or perhaps I rang him – and I told him Riccarda had left London for good. (I had never yet admitted to him we had been lovers.) The job I was doing didn't suit me. I found it frightening to teach twenty people how to read and write, and going out on the street or taking public transport made me anxious. I was looking after my parents' flat while they were away, very tired, I didn't sleep well and my voice and hands shook often. I didn't tell him any of that, just that things hadn't worked out quite the way I planned. I hadn't gone back to university to complete my PhD, because I hadn't got the second grant I applied for: without it, I couldn't afford the time or the fee.

Two days later, Marco was at my doorstep.

'Hey! I'm here to cheer you up.'

I spent the night talking to him over two bottles of red wine and then a half-bottle of whisky, talking in a way I never had before. By the time we were done with drinking and talking I was so drunk I didn't remember what either of us had said.

For the next two days, we went wandering around London as if we hadn't talked at all, looking for our old haunts and finding some of them gone – a cinema in South Kensington, a Chinese café in Bloomsbury.

'You know, I thought you were going to celebrate your freedom and give me a great time in London. Treat me like a superstar. I thought we'd at least have fun. Instead, you're treating me like an acquaintance. Or a stranger. And if you were entertaining a stranger, you would be doing more for him. Actually, London is boring. There's so little to do.'

He was laughing, but he meant it.

I had been surprised and pleased to see him, but now I didn't even know if I was really glad he'd come.

On the third evening, on the terrace of a pub by the banks of the Thames in Chelsea, we sat down together over pints of icy lager, facing the river and a houseboat, and he said: 'I have to talk to you. I so wanted to see you I just took the first plane. I wanted to help you. Instead your moods are dragging me down. You know, Mehran? I don't want much from life. Never have done. I just want to finish my doctorate and get a job at my old university, and if I can, to travel back to India and earn enough to keep myself going. I want to love and be loved. But you? You're a promising poet, but you keep your poems in a notebook. You suffer like an artist, like one of those romantic heroes in the poems we used to study, but instead of doing anything with your poetry, you're living bad verse. Instead of celebrating your freedom, you're mourning for something you never wanted or even had. Wake up, Mehran. The dream's over. I won't stand by and watch you lose yourself like this. I can't. I don't think you even want me here.'

His words were harsh, yet underscored by something desperate. I almost said that he had always disapproved of Riccarda, that he'd perhaps been jealous because I had had something he didn't have, and he wanted to sully it. Or maybe he had come to London wanting to confide in me about something, had done so, perhaps, on that drunk and forgotten night of confidences, and had expected some response from me. I didn't say much. Perhaps I said just enough to let him know my doubts. Or else he heard what I hadn't said.

I turned my back to hide my expression.

'I'm leaving, Mehran,' he said with his hand on my shoulder.

I didn't say anything, didn't follow him.

When I went home – an hour later? – the sky was very black, in the way it sometimes is on October nights, and he was there, sitting on the doorstep, waiting for me to let him into my apartment.

In the morning, he woke me up. 'I'm off. Just saying goodbye. Don't get out of bed. By the way, you remember? I owe you fifty pounds.'

He rode back to Italy in the back of a lorry with a load of vegetables, days earlier than he had planned to. He left his return ticket on my desk with the money he said he owed me. It was roughly half, in sterling, of the rupees I'd lent him in Agra.

1983

My life didn't change overnight, but the work was regular. And just as the tutor whose work I had taken over for a year was coming back, and I was going to be out of two jobs, I heard from Dominic that my old university was recruiting graduates to give private tuition to part-time students. At first the work was sporadic and the cheques slow to come in, but I made a living which, in time, became decent, if frugal.

1984

I worked during the day and my evenings were free. The irony was that I owed the jobs I was doing to my knowledge of my mother tongue, but it wasn't Dick's florid disquisitions on lyric poetry that guided me: I had acquired the discipline I applied to my knowledge of verbs, nouns, clauses, conditionals and subjunctives from Lady L and her textbooks of Persian grammar.

1985

Everything seemed to happen through chance meetings in the campus courtyard. I ran into Sujit there,
an old friend of Marco's, who offered me a job: com-
missioning books and music reviews, and subediting,
for a journal of South Asian diasporic culture called
Aangan he was receiving public funds to run. 'The
work will take a day or two a week,' he said. 'You
can do a lot of it at home.'

1986

Back on the campus of my old university I was reminded, from time to time, that I had once belonged to the enchanted confraternity of the former students of Lady L. I smiled and never explained that I had only studied with her for a few months, and away from class her interest lay not in aesthetics or prosody but in the economic demography of Qajar Iran. My limited knowledge of Persian poetry was self-acquired. Academic legend was turning Lady L into a Hafiz-quoting mystic. A side of her I had certainly never seen. But there were other stories in circulation too, about how she'd been a spy, and the evil mastermind behind the fall of Mossadegh in 1953.

It's easy enough to live with a legend. I was briefly the flower in her buttonhole and the star of her eye, so I didn't think I was being deceitful, or posing as one of her enchanted circle. I had just forgotten how short my time with her had

been, and that she only taught me the austerity
of Persian's grammatical rules and nothing at all
about poetry.

IV

Love Poison

Khatm hoti hai zindagani aaj
khaak men milti hai javani aaj
chup raho kyun abas bhi rote ho
muft kahe ko jaan khote ho
samjho is shab ko shab baraat ki raat
ham hain mehmaan tumhare raat ki raat
chain dil ko na aayega tujh bin
ab ke bicchre milenge hashr ke din …

My life comes to an end today
So why must you waste your years without gain
and fling your youth into the dust?
Silence, love! Why do you weep in vain?
Think of these last hours as our night of
celebration.
Until day breaks I'll be your guest
Without you I will never be at rest:
(For once we're parted, we won't meet again till
judgement day.)

From Zehr-i-Ishq, *by Shauq*

Many years later, a friend looks at Mehran's album of photographs and says: 'You changed as you grew older. In your twenties, you look out on the world in a way that's both trusting and seductive. Your body's relaxed, yet you seem poised to fly. The photographs of your thirties are reticent. Edgy. Tense, as if you're withdrawing from the camera's eye. Witholding yourself. Your face changed. And your posture. What happened?'

I study images of Mehran. Alone in a park, running, reading, poised to climb a tree. Slender, with a sharp jawline, strong teeth, thick untidy black hair which he has attempted to tame with gel. Smiling at the face behind a camera. A young man captured forever in a lover's gaze.

1987

There's a later picture in the album, with a date pencilled in the lower right hand corner: July 1987. The man, in profile, in a blue and white shirt with cropped sleeves; brown, smiling, nibbling a woman's ear. She's laughing. Dressed in red, hair very short, she's dark, voluptuous. Happy.

He remembers her dancing the first time they met. She's tall, dark-skinned, dressed in black, a short dress like a T-shirt, revealing long brown legs. She's dancing to sax music, swaying in an unchoreographed way, swaying like a tree. Then someone changes the music and plays a desert melody, high sweet male voices over a wind instrument, jangling mandolin, two sets of drums. Her movements change. She's slower, her head moves from side to side, her arms are sinuous above her head, her wrists twine around each other in a series of deft, subtle movements. This is something, he thinks, she's been doing since childhood: not learned, but absorbed and part of her, at variance with her short hair, her short dress. Then, suddenly, she sways, falls. Everyone in the room rushes towards her. But before anyone reaches her she's up, and laughing. A choreographed fall?

He's invited to a birthday party by an old friend and it happens to be at Marvi's house, just a short walk away on Clifton Hill.

She greets him at the door.

'Mehran.'

'I know. I used to see you at the café by the canal. I know your girlfriend, slightly. Did she mention me? Marvi Ansari.'

'Ah, yes … Like Umar's Marvi?'

'Ha-a! Few people know *that* story. My name's actually Mariam, but I prefer Marvi. I'm Sindhi. Or my father is. My husband's called Umar Sumro too. You're Sindhi?'

'Half.'

'How's Ayla?'

'In America. She left last autumn.'

'I know. But … what news? Is she surviving the Midwest? Or shouldn't I be asking?'

She has light brown eyes and cropped black hair.

'Didn't you know?' he says. 'Ayla's in Santa Barbara. She got married last week.'

He stays all night, after everyone leaves, talking to her till first light. Her voice is deep, she drawls. When he says goodbye she kisses his mouth in the doorway. She tastes of cigarettes.

He's back at her house the next evening, listening to music, singing the words of Faiz or Ghalib, drinking iced vodka; again, he leaves at dawn.

The third day she comes to visit him at nearly midnight, on her way home from dinner with friends at a restaurant.

A migrant from Karachi like him, Marvi is, at twenty-eight, four years younger than Mehran. She's an economist. The mother of infant twins, and married: unhappily, he soon finds out. She came to London with her husband, did her PhD at the London School of Economics, and took up a postdoctoral Research Fellowship when she finished. She's reworking her doctoral dissertation into a book; it's a rereading of Joan Robinson in the context of Marvi's native Sindh where she did her research, wearing a chadar, in small, conservative towns. (Even Mehran, with his non-existent knowledge of economic theory, can appreciate her work when he dips into the bound manuscript she lends him.) Moving away from Karachi means living away from her husband, who has gone home to look after his estates.

At seven, Marvi was sent to a convent school in Murree and then on to a boarding school in Cheshire, where she was known as Mary. (She learned to rebel – at being served sausages and bacon, for example – and the appellation had become Contrary Mary.) She struggled with her family as a teenager when she ran away from Cambridge with a vagabond actor, but then she married a distant cousin she said had fallen in love with her at a family gathering, went back to complete her studies at LSE, and laid fresh claim to her father's affection.

Mehran is envious when she speaks of the sense of belonging to which she clings by going back, every year and sometimes more often, to Karachi, or to the small feudal town in Sindh where she spent childhood summers with loving maternal grandparents.

'I spend my life longing for the place I'm not in, but when I go back I never fit,' she laments. 'I married a place, not a man, because I thought the man was home.'

He knows what she means, though he's been back to India only twice and never returned to Karachi, his birthplace. He prefers to wander outwards: home, if there's any such place, is with the people who love him. And that, at the time he meets Marvi, is Rome, where Riccarda has been living for five years. He has begun to feel, after the Indian trips, that he doesn't belong anywhere; he's no longer in thrall to the places of his past.

He has only known Marvi a month when, at summer's end, he hears she's had an accident – a fall, down a slope – on a day trip to the Chilterns. One leg is badly damaged; she is told it might have to be amputated. She'll have to suspend her Fellowship, her promising academic career, for a year, at least. Mehran is on holiday too, at Riccarda's house by the sea, outside Rome.

Back in London, he spends hours at Marvi's hospital bedside; then he's on call for days and days when she comes home. How, he wonders, did they bring her to London? She's enmeshed in a tangle of wires, can barely move; but she tells stories, laughs, sings.

'The last thing I remember about my fall', she tells him, 'is a heather-like plant tickling my left nostril while most of my life flashed before my eyes like an unfolding screen.'

He's never been good at tending the bedridden or the ill, but he tries.

For a time he thinks he loves her. Love makes it all worthwhile, the dull hours at work, the distance from every unanswered prayer. He even thinks they are happy. What they share, though, is only the illusion of happiness waiting.

1988

'But who are you to me? Are we a couple?' she cries.

What can he say? They haven't given what they have a name. She hadn't wanted to declare a relationship until she decided on divorce, as she's about to claim a hefty alimony. And he's stopped asking about the future, the thought of which frightens him more and more.

From the first encounter of their bodies, they were always tentative, hasty lovers – it was her manner, as if a drunken, furtive loving, in inappropriate and uncomfortable places, in a welter of half-discarded clothes, assuaged the sense of guilt that fulfilled desire seemed to give her. But by now, a little more than a year after they met, they have almost ceased to touch each other. Lovemaking, at least in the conventional sense, has become an ordeal for her.

But from time to time she still reaches out to him

for warmth. He holds her thin body with its fragile bones in his arms for hours, kisses her face or her bared skin all over, until his body rebels against the constraints of hers and then she cries and says she knows he has to go elsewhere for the pleasure that she can no longer give him; one day, she knows, he'll leave her for a saner, stronger woman.

After the accident, Marvi had a period of what seemed to be a total, even miraculous, recovery: she walked, travelled home, even went back to lecture at university. In the winter months while she healed they worked together for days on her manuscript, which a university press had accepted for publication. Then, at an alcohol-laden party in Karachi, where she had flown to for the winter against her doctor's advice, she fell again. After that, she always walked with a stick, which became an essential part of her flamboyant party performances.

At conferences, she made glamorous appearances on platforms, dressed in black with a black cane; but her oddly fragmented, aggressive and occasionally incoherent lectures and interventions soon made her very unpopular with listeners and organisers alike. Whether drink, drugs, nerves or pain caused that behaviour Mehran couldn't tell, but after one or two such episodes, he refused to go to public events with her. Later, he hears that she attends conferences in the wheelchair she often uses as a passport to service from others; she loudly heckles speakers, usually right-wing economists, from the audience. At other times, she lies in bed for months.

He has watched her seek relief from constant pain: wine; vodka; cocktails of painkillers (at first, after her accident, a nurse injected her with morphine, but then Marvi persuaded her unscrupulous GP to allow her to use the needle herself). Sometimes she starts drinking as soon as she gets out of bed, until she falls asleep at some odd time of the day, wakes up after an hour or two, has a few gulps of black coffee, and then it's back to the bottle, to the vodka or the wine.

Though he has tried to help, he isn't strong enough. He feels he is drowning. He drinks more than he should when he's with her; sometimes when he's not, he drinks to escape from whatever it is that keeps him from leaving her. But drinking, he feels, is merely a kind of slow suicide: people who want to kill themselves should just do it, swiftly, not waste time over it. He turns abstemious for days, which she says is his contrary way of keeping control and shutting her out.

'But who are you to me? Are we a couple?' she cries. 'Sometimes you make me feel I'm less than a woman. Much less. You're cold, Mehran.'

What can he say?

She cries, kohl streaks her cheeks. It's New Year's Eve; he wants to leave her, to celebrate with others, elsewhere.

They fight and he stays away, goes back to his parents' home in St John's Wood, to rest, to hide.

When Mehran is with his parents, his father so obviously avoids talking about Marvi that at some point Mehran finds himself mentioning her. His mother hardly speaks without naming Marvi. The few friends he has left – looking back, he will remember no faces, only kind, if disapproving, voices – tell him he's the giver in an unequal relationship. He responds (and her own words would endorse this) that they are an equal part of that horseshoe pattern, a movement that leads them back and then away, back and then away from each other.

She has told him so many lies – about her marriage, her friends, her plans – that he now doubts his perception of her.

And of himself. Or he sees himself through her eyes.

Sometimes he longs for the clove taste of her mouth, the tea smell of her underarms when she's hot or aroused. But the tastes and the smells are lost in some broken yesterday. He no longer wants to make love to her. She doesn't desire him.

When he tries to escape her he feels drained, empty; it takes him days to refill himself. Most often he succumbs to her calls, when she drives his parents half mad by ringing at two in the morning, or when she tells him that if she can't see him, she'll over-medicate. He goes back. Because he's too tired for anything or anyone else. Because he has told her so much about himself that she's the only one he can share his secrets with, even if she'll use them as a whip to flay him, rip his skin. Because he's afraid of emptiness.

He can keep away from her for a day, a week, a fortnight. But then his own ambivalent needs, his loneliness, draw him back.

1989

Another photograph is marked 31 December 1988. It's of a man in a grey sweater over a black shirt, his hair cropped short. A woman in a thin beige dress, her face pale, her cheekbones prominent, her black hair disordered, sitting on his knee. Their smiles reveal them as the couple from the earlier photograph, but a careful look shows the changes in both. His expression is staged, as if he's hiding something, a backache, perhaps. His lips stretch to show even white teeth. His hair is thinning. The woman's smile reveals dark gums; her eyeliner has smudged around her enormous, frightened eyes.

'I thought two vulnerable people like Marvi and I could trust each other, give the other what each lacked. Now', he tells Riccarda on New Year's Day, in a Pont Street flat she's rented for a season, 'I don't know what my worst mistake was: the trust, or the sharing of the lack.'

'Have you thought of the fine line between love and kindness?' Riccarda asks him. 'You're a kind person, one of the kindest I know, but kindness needs detachment, darling. And pity. Kindness is what you think that girl might need, and you're most probably right, but you must also understand pity's not what she wants. What's more important to me: is she kind to you?'

Riccarda's homes – the Roman apartment, the rented service flats in Chelsea and South Kensington – are his only refuge. To her love of Broadway musicals, Riccarda has added an obsession with fantasy films of every kind (she insists they are allegories): *Star Wars, Flash Gordon, Conan the Barbarian, Dune, Ladyhawk*. They spend hours at the cinema, or watching videos. In Riccarda's company, he pretends to forget Marvi. For a while.

April. During the Easter break, Mehran decides he wants to spend his thirty-fourth birthday in Rome, with Riccarda. But Marvi begins to weep: her birthday's a day after his, she's going to be thirty. Hasn't he thought she would miss him, how much she'd need him? He delays his trip to the end of the month, stays on in London. The party, supposed to be a surprise, is arranged at a Polynesian restaurant in a Mayfair hotel. He arrives at 9.30 pm, in a suit, takes his place at the table she's meant to be at, among her distant cousins. She isn't there yet; he eats alone, with near-strangers. She appears at midnight. Dressed in transparent silver. With a couple of college friends in tow. They couldn't get her to leave the bar where they stopped off on the way for a cocktail. She's drunk.

Sometimes Mehran sees colleagues for a drink after work, and sometimes they invite him home to dinner. He rarely goes out with Marvi, who won't meet Mehran's friends except in his house or hers. She showed up drunk (or drugged – it's hard to tell with her) at his place more than twice. At least once she turned away some friends of Mehran's after asking them over to dinner. Now he always eats with friends from work at restaurants: they feel awkward about asking him to their homes on his own. They assume that he's spoken for; he's no good at filling the empty space at their tables for an eligible man to pair off with a single female guest. To such acquaintances, most of them in long-term relationships, he is an anomaly: neither single, divorced, nor committed. A man not even in his mid-thirties with a mysterious woman in the background: a sick woman, as rumour has it. 'Perhaps she's uneducated, or in purdah, how would you know?' he sometimes feels like saying.

Marvi has many friends. When Mehran first met her, she was surrounded by Third World intellectuals of the sort that debated world politics: some, or so they claimed, were so far to the left that they felt it was pointless to revolt, because they couldn't fight such a rotten system. They found Mehran bourgeois: he signed petitions, marched in protests and for causes, had even voted for Kinnock. Several of them seemed to share a predilection for Bollywood movies, noisy, violent and very different from the lachrymose romances he watched as an adolescent. They thought these Ayn Rand-like fantasies of heroic villains and virtuous whores were a genuine expression of the popular spirit; the only way, apart from street theatre, to make authentic art in the Third World. He kept away from them; he didn't like armchair politics.

Other friends were rich Pakistanis of the kind he had grown up with and learned to avoid. Her friends were vitally important to her and they decided early to keep their circles separate. Then, as her drinking grew more dangerous, and she spent long afternoons at home, she took to making friends at the corner shop, the beautician's, and most often at local pubs. It isn't uncommon for her to invite him to dinner and for him to enter a crowded flat, immerse himself in a fug of dope, the stench of burnt food, and the blare of Bollywood music from her ghetto blaster. (Though she loved traditional Pakistani music when they first met, it's always Bollywood now.) If he leaves early, he's subjected to screaming midnight calls: 'You're a man, you walked away, you should have thrown them out.' If he stays, he is accused of insulting her friends with his intellectual arrogance, while she – so much better educated, with her doctorate, than Mehran – can mingle with the masses.

For a while, a succession of young women – Tisha, Fifi and Lili – encircle her, borrow her make-up, wear her knickers, take her earrings and her money. And then there are young men. Students and struggling artists, who are with her at all times, carrying her parcels, making her joints, fetching her bottles, ampoules and needles, pouring her drinks. If, as she says (and for the longest while he believes her), he is the most important presence in her life, then why this constant need for others? He stays silent, but once he protests when one of her young men, a Swiss-German acolyte of Osho who calls himself Hanuman, pasty-faced, small and hairy in a vest and shorts, indicates that Mehran is unwanted.

Yet the vaguest suspicion that someone else may lay claim to any part of his affections turns Marvi's voice into a howling wind in the branches of a tall tree, and her body into a weeping willow. He has become almost superstitious about mentioning anyone in his life to her, female or even male. Strangely, suddenly, whoever he becomes close to disappears from his world if she chances to meet them. That he can understand. She is gracious, and when she wants to, she can create an aura of beauty and utter charm around herself; but she is manifestly, regally possessive. One of her habits, on the rare occasions they meet friends in her flat, is to hand him some object, a lighter or a watch or a chain, and mention that he had been searching for it that morning on his way to work. Or she leaves some garment on a sofa where he seems to have abandoned it (he has a habit of slinging sweaters over his shoulders and leaving them, and all his other things, wherever he puts them down). It appears he lives with her, or sleeps there more often than he does, which is nearly never. He knows she hides his things, to do this. Just once, he says: 'That lighter isn't mine, and you know I wasn't at your house this morning.' She winces. The friend he's with tells him: 'You embarrassed both me and Marvi; you should have let it pass.'

What makes him afraid, at times, is his feeling that he has only to mention a relationship, a future prospect, a trip – anything, in short, that might take him away from her – for it to be blighted by her jealousy, bound to go wrong.

'You reach a point and an age where it's hard to find someone other than your current mate, even if you're looking,' Lilla writes. 'Who do we find that's custom made for us? It becomes harder to meet people, and our standards and expectations rise as we grow older. We turn more and more to each other for companionship, we solitaries, but friends don't keep you warm at night.'

But he isn't, or has stopped, looking for someone to warm him. He has decided, since he met Marvi, that he will never have children. Each new love, if you can even call it that, is a replacement for an old, lost feeling: after meeting Marvi, he knows that anyone who finds a place in his life is a surrogate for something he has never known or had, or an escape from someone else; from an inadequacy in his own ability to take or to give. He isn't made to be a lover: a husband, even less. At some point he can't locate, restlessness has become his real companion, closer to him than anyone he has ever known.

He teaches for fifteen, sometimes twenty hours a week – he is, again, teaching large groups on Mondays and Thursdays, and also an Indian History module to undergraduates. He's often too tired to do anything but read a few pages of a novel in the evenings. His employment still counts as part-time and that's what he is, in every way, a part-timer: part-time language instructor, part-time historian, part-time editor, part-time lover. His job at the university, though he's a dutiful and conscientious teacher, is only a job, and he would have been as diligent at any other. He's given up most of his magazine work to younger colleagues, more angry, more hungry; he only writes the occasional inconsequential article. He's thirty-four; at thirty-three, his great-uncle Rafi had published about twenty stories and died.

For two decades he's been away from a city that

he left without a backward glance. His life in that rainless place of his birth was filled with a longing for rainy places: but now that he lives in a city where it rains all year, he dreams of the desert and the sea, and the smell of warm raindrops on wet earth. He wants another, redder moon, longer days in winter, and in summer an early, flagrant sunset.

Dear R,

My mother told us: never try to make pets of wild creatures, like peacocks or deer; they yearn for their wild places, and their longing brings bad luck to their captors. But who holds me captive, and in what hunter's net? I remember the images of the poem my mother used to recite so long ago, Kalidasa's poem about the cloud messenger, carrying love messages back from a man in exile to the city where he'd left behind his beloved, letters of infinite longing. And I, too, want to send such messages home on the back of a rain cloud, those messages about the net that I'm trapped in, trapped like the peacock who had only wanted to escape captivity when he heard the rain fall, smelled the earth's longing, listened to his playmates' cries. But I have nowhere to send my messages to: only the rainless place in which I am a stranger now. I too have built myself a net of words and images in lieu of a home.

Other people's words. And sometimes I imagine myself escaping that net: rising as vapour then dissolving and dripping away, drop by drop, to become not the exile who sends the messages, but the cloud that carries them, to rain down my longings on the dry, dry earth of my past, the land I left behind.

Your loving M.

In December, with the days drawn in and the sleet and the rain coming down in murky sheets, he thinks about that other rain, and the rainless city of his past; of the odd yearnings for greener landcapes he had throughout his childhood in that rainless place. He picks up his old black notebook, in which he had written regularly until he started teaching. He writes for a day or two, or rather a night or three. He writes about his parents and their garden, about the sound of songs and the rain. He's always found it hard to give his yearnings a shape, and when Marvi reads it she says: 'It's beautiful and nostalgic, but autobiographical writing is a bourgeois indulgence that doesn't take the reader anywhere and neither does your piece. Overflow is what this is, just a novice writer's confessional overflow. Stick to translating poetry, you're good at that. You're an interpreter of other people's words.'

He knows all that. He lives in a fragile shelter,

and when the rain comes, it might collapse. He doesn't have an imagination. He long ago squandered the small poetic capital he had on the handful of excerpts he translated from 'The Poison of Love' for the *Journal of Urdu Literature*; since then, his lyrical urge has left him. But when he wrote down those memories, it was as if he recognised that one day he would have to be a messenger to himself, carrying stories from the places of his past to his present place, and back again from present to past. Whether they make sense to anyone else or not, he needs them to find himself a form, build a vehicle for his longing.

Not yet, though. He isn't ready.

He puts away the notebook in a drawer with his other scribblings.

1990

Riccarda is going to be operated on for a sudden, rapacious cancer of the lung nearly seven years after she left London to live in Rome. Ironically, it was diagnosed just after her son found a job in a prestigious New York law firm, and she finally decided to leave the mysterious Mr Santini for ever.

Mehran tells Marvi the news. He places his head on the back of the sofa and shuts his eyes. She touches him. 'I'm sorry, so sorry.' He weeps as he hasn't wept since he was an infant. Marvi runs her fingers through his thinning hair and gently tugs its roots in an odd, consoling way, relieving the tautness of his scalp. He's grateful for her sympathy but he feels trapped, in himself, in his skull and in his bones, unable to reach out to her, unable to feel her.

The first time he speaks to Riccarda on the phone after her operation she is under sedation and says: '*Ti voglio molto bene, amore.*' That ambiguous phrase – *I care for you, I wish you well, I love you* – that's oddly so close to Urdu, and can be used by siblings, friends and lovers. Later, she doesn't remember the call, or what she said.

He travels to meet Riccarda in Rome. Disease has made her thin and incandescent. She looks so ethereal people stop and stare at her in the street; children want to touch her.

In the Missoni shop near the Spanish Steps, where she insists on buying him an expensively elegant sweater, the saleswoman looks from Mehran to her and remarks: 'Your son looks so like you!'

'I think so too,' Riccarda says.

Outside, she asks: 'Do you remember the way we were, love? That summer …?'

He kisses her hand. They've never, ever, since they parted, talked about that time. Their time.

Back to London. Marvi, in one of her rages. Her wrists and arms covered in dull red scratches.

'You're obsessed with Riccarda, with her cancer, it's separating you from your friends and all those who used to love you. I know you think I'm crazy. But you're a fucking ghost.'

After the news of Riccarda's illness, Marvi and Mehran have less and less to say to one another. Her flat is filled with the friends she meets at pubs and bars: they spend their evenings around her, smoking hashish or marijuana, taking ecstasy and drinking. And Mehran is with her less and less; more and more often he's in his own studio flat a few streets away, at calling distance.

At less than thirty-five, he feels like a cloud, like the ghost Marvi calls him, as if he died in some other era. He has become used to being unfulfilled, and even if he does find himself in other beds it doesn't matter. He is still Marvi's. He is still alone.

Dear R,

Once Marvi said to me, her head resting on my knee, in one of her drug-dazed moments: 'When I was in Karachi in July, it started to rain and didn't stop for three days. There was no electricity and the streets were flooded. I watched the clouds gather and burst, and the lightning flash and the rain beat against my window, fight it as if it had a will to smash the glass barrier and break in, break in and wash over me, drown me, and I thought the memory of you was like that rain, and I was that window, with invisible bars and invisible shutters, and the more you wanted to smash the glass I'd raise the barriers and you'd be like that rain, with its flashing and its storming, and then its sudden end when it's spent itself ...'

Your loving M.

1991

In the world beyond their windows, things have also changed, some for the better: since Benazir Bhutto came into power, even the disappointments that pursued her supporters during her first term didn't succeed in vanquishing hopes for a new era in Pakistan. Many of their friends are going back; Mehran, too, begins to dream of his lost city. In response to the burgeoning national promise, he has started reading contemporary Urdu writing; his interest has turned from his earlier field of study to post-partition literature, the prose writers that were the intellectual progeny of Faiz, his favourite modern poet. Now he wants to teach today's Urdu fiction and poetry, translate it and write about it, at least for the next ten years. He spends hours in the university library, searching out uncut, unread volumes of fiction and poetry freshly arrived from Pakistan.

Events in Iraq take him, with protesting

Londoners, into the winter streets, denouncing all wars and the new empires that wage them. In the early evenings, if he escapes the library, he sometimes meets a colleague for a drink in the Senior Common Room or a small friendly pub nearby, which serves fish and chips at suppertime. He doesn't go back to his empty flat until ten or eleven at night.

Marco hasn't been back to London since that curtailed summer visit in 1982, but, after a gap of six years, Mehran had seen him twice, though very briefly, on visits to Rome in the late eighties. Marco had acted as if nothing had ever gone wrong between them, and had wanted Mehran to stay with him for a few nights. Mehran was friendly but busy, and once actually forgot to call Marco after promising to let him know if he could spend a day or two with him.

When he rings up from Rome to say he's attending a conference on Iqbal and the Concept of the Self at the School of Oriental and African Studies, Mehran hasn't seen or spoken to him for at least two years. Marco asks if he can stay. He arrives on a mild July evening and phones from a payphone near Mehran's house. He got off at the wrong stop and lost his way. Mehran goes to meet him, finds him not far from the Regent's Canal, near Lisson Grove. The sky is darkening, but Mehran sees Marco in the distance. He hasn't changed much over the years, but something about his air makes Mehran understand more easily why people once found him plain and now call him handsome. His spare frame has filled out, he wears contact lenses, and his longish hair is brushed with grey; his once edgy manner is expansive, tactile. He dresses in baggy, elegant clothes that conceal his slight belly; he has travelled to places – Cambodia, Thailand, Bali – that seem only peripherally connected to the academic pursuits to which he is still dedicated. He had moved to Venice, married a Tamilian he'd once introduced Mehran to in Rome where she was living then with a musician friend of his; they have a daughter, but now seem to be involved in acrimony over property and custody.

'I live like a hermit now,' Marco says. 'No money, no home, and half a job. How are you?' But he seems comfortable, if not affluent; he still has that particular Italian rootedness that intrigues Mehran: roots in a country and a city he's lived in most of his life, surrounded by faces he has known since his childhood; places – lakes, beaches, cemeteries, streets – he goes back to for solace; a native language he lives in, that inhabits him.

'Well,' Mehran says, 'you know, quite well, all said and done. Reading around, in search of textual satisfaction. Work's steady, that helps.'

On the streets he has known for twenty years, Mehran feels like a drifting cloud: so light, so weightless, he must be invisible. Some nights his blankets weigh heavy on his skin; when he lays his head down on a pillow it's like a stone resting on a stone. From time to time he is possessed with a longing for something he's never known; though he might call it nostalgia or homesickness, he knows it's not: a longing that makes him restless at times, at others listless. He can tell Marvi about it all; she understands, though it hurts her, and she uses it against Mehran in her rages, it's their only lasting bond, this listlessness, the restlessness. But he can't tell Marco these things.

Marco behaves, from the first hour, as if they've never been apart.

'I saw Dick this afternoon,' he recounts over a glass of whisky in the university bar they sometimes met at in their university days, after his day at the Iqbal conference. 'He's writing a book about his adventures with boys in Lucknow. Wrestlers and masseurs! No wonder he loved Mir's gay *masnavis* so much.' He chortles at his own quip.

Marvi insists on inviting them to dinner, to a very expensive Chinese restaurant that looks like a blue brothel. As usual, she makes a very late appearance; but she's mildly tipsy, not really drunk yet. She proceeds to drink most of two bottles of wine with her food, and stubs out cigarettes in her plate, but her conversation remains witty and ranges wide. She leaves a huge tip, in cash. She insists, later, on walking home between them, hanging on to their arms, and forces them to come up for a drink. By the time they leave, she's made Mehran promise to have her over to dinner the next evening. It's a Thursday, and he's teaching; but she says she'll come late, after nine.

'Seems like a difficult girl,' Marco says on the way back to Mehran's flat. 'Troubled. Very bright, though.'

On his way to the airport, Marco says he has something to confess.

'About Marvi and me. You know we'd all arranged to meet for supper when you got home at nine? I let myself in with your key to wait for you. I fell asleep on the sofa with the TV on and assumed you were back early when the bell rang at seven. It was Marvi: she arrived much earlier than expected, said she's made a mistake about the time and thought it was eight. I was left alone with her for two hours. She insisted on opening the bottle of champagne she'd brought with her. She sat beside me and kissed me and touched me till I was on fire. When you came back early from your evening class, I heard the bell ring twice, and I pushed her away, hard, so she tripped and twisted her wrist. I was helping her up when you came in and we said she'd fallen.'

Mehran doesn't really understand the story, the

timings, the blurred detail. It's true, Marco was helping Marvi up from the floor when he had come in, but Marvi trips and falls often. He knows Marvi will tell him her own version of events, say that Marco made advances to her, attacked her when she refused him.

'It hardly matters. What you don't understand, Marco, is that I'm the one who has to live with her complaints.'

Marco has reached South Kensington, where he has to change trains for Heathrow. Mehran doesn't remember later if he had planned to go all the way to the airport, but says goodbye to Marco on the Piccadilly Line platform. When Marco puts out his arms to embrace him, Mehran just pats his shoulder, moves away with a few abrupt words, doesn't look back.

Mehran walks out on Marvi in anger a few weeks after Marco's visit. Not because Marvi has found someone else; Mehran hasn't, either. Not because of her drugs and her drinking (though Mehran found six empty bottles of vodka in her kitchen after four days of being away from her at a conference in Leyden). But because she's lied to him too often. Because it's all dead.

After some months of silence Marco makes a stoned late-night call. He asks about Marvi. Mehran is willing to forget, but Marco is obviously embarrassed and trying to put things right.

'You're both wonderful people. But so, so wrong for each other ...'

'It's over, Marco.'

Mehran doesn't want to explain. That's all he says.

1992

Mid-December. On a silver-blue morning soon after her fifty-ninth birthday, Mehran takes a trip with Riccarda. They are on San Francesco's trail; in the span of a single day, they visit Gubbio and Assisi. Many years ago, they had seen Dario Fo at London's Riverside Theatre, reading a monologue he had written about the saint. In Fo's version, Francesco was not only an animal-loving man of peace, but a clown, a subversive, God's jester. Who better to visit his shrine with than Riccarda, the musician and cradle Catholic? Mehran, lazily mystic rather than religious (but resolutely Muslim), is entranced by the day; by Assisi, by the tomb's tranquility. He lights a candle, shuts his eyes and prays for Riccarda's health as he would at the shrine of a Sufi saint.

1993

An April morning. Lilla phones at dawn. She's ringing, Mehran thinks, with belated birthday greetings.

She says: 'Be strong. She's dead.'

He's been wondering why Riccarda didn't call on his birthday a few days before, as she always does. 'She lived like a warrior,' someone says: 'She didn't give up fighting, even at the end.' But she forgot her Italian and her English in her last days, and spoke only Spanish.

Neither Lilla nor Mehran go to her funeral.

O cuore! Congedati, e vivi.

He spends some weeks in silence.

Then Lilla calls again. 'Come over to Rome. Take the next flight you can get. We can talk about her, spend a little time together.'

Mehran hesitates.

She says: 'I'll drive you to Assisi. Have our own memorial for her. She'd like that.'

Mehran books a flight and flies out two days later.

When Mehran reaches Rome, he calls Marco – on impulse, or from a sense of duty to the past, he doesn't remember why. Marco drives over immediately to pick him up.

'I'm sorry. I don't really know what to say. I know how much she meant to you.'

Somewhere in his eyes, Mehran thinks, *Marco must hold a picture of me, as the young man who fell so briefly in love, and a memory of the woman I loved then, though he never liked her.*

They're in the Monte Mario flat Marco has borrowed from his parents, with whom, until recently, he had been living in Frascati after his marriage fell apart. He sits there, opposite Mehran, as the night wears on, drinking wine and smoking Marlboros, shirtless and in shorts, his eyes threaded with red, his large hands with their short fingers resting palm upwards on his bare knees, and he tells Mehran, again, in a hot torrent of broken phrases, how Marvi had propositioned him in Mehran's sitting room that evening on his last trip, before he left London.

Mehran remembers the evening only vaguely; he

has a clearer recollection of Marvi's version. He also knows about the games Marvi played to make him feel hurt or angry, or anything at all. He's ceased to care.

To Marco, as he spills out his stories over red wine, Mehran must seem quiet and distracted. Mehran wants only to talk about Riccarda: he waits for a pause, tries to tell Marco about the last time he saw her, and what she said about Marvi.

Marco breaks in. Begins to shout. 'You destroyed her, you know. You always do. You're the coldest and most narcissistic man I've ever known. You can never have a real relationship, you aren't capable of that, you were attached for years to the apron strings of a sick woman who summoned you to entertain her when she was bored and always took advantage of you, and now you're obsessed with her ghost. Very convenient. And what you've played at all these years with Marvi, also a walking – or should I say limping – disaster, is a vicarious, virtual game. I'm not shocked that she walked out on you; even her betrayals were only attempts to bring down your walls of ice. Do you know the effect you have on people? You freeze them …'

'Marco, shut up.'

'You know what? I enjoyed her advances, because I wanted to know what you saw in her. That's why I kissed her. You know what she did that night? Just as you rang the bell, she offered to …'

'I don't want to hear any of this. You're paralytic.'

Marco leans over and grabs Mehran's shoulders, as if he's about to shake him. Mehran smells his sweat, the red wine and smoke on his breath. Then suddenly his grip slackens; his hands go up to Mehran's face, firm palms stroking, holding Mehran's jaw, fingertips tapping Mehran's cheekbones.

'*Sai che ti voglio tanto bene.*'

For a moment Mehran is too stunned to move. Then he shakes Marco off and gets up to leave, feeling unsteady himself. He has always hated red wine.

Marco slumps in his chair; doesn't offer to drive Mehran back to Trastevere, which is just as well, because he's been drinking so much, and smoking hashish too. Mehran should be drunk too, but as he walks down the street he only feels cold in the mild night weather; his eyes are stinging from lack of sleep.

Marco seems to be unhappy. His way of speaking is often ponderous, pedantic. Along with the Tantric philosophy he's been endlessly researching, he's attending sessions on psychosynthesis or some such arcane discipline that casts shadows in the oddest angles of his life, including the fragile corner of his friendship with Mehran.

Mehran hadn't really wanted to see him; he knew that Marco and he were no longer the way they once had been, that he'd probably come away from their encounter wistful and disappointed.

But he hadn't expected to leave the way he is now, shaken, trembling, more affected by the loss of Riccarda than he'd been when Lilla first gave him the news. He's talking to Marco in his head, wishing he'd reminded him: *I was the one who walked out on Marvi in cold anger; even when she gave me an ultimatum I never turned back.* But perhaps there had been no turning. The last time Mehran walked away Marvi only called out to him once. And then he heard, with relief, that she'd gone to live in Karachi.

Long ago, Mehran learned not to think about the people he's been parted from, except with the vaguest feelings of affection or nostalgia. Now he'll erase memories of all the hurtful, angry partings; he'll eradicate their presence from his life.

He takes a couple of buses to get back to Lilla's place at dawn. They plan to leave early, for Assisi.

'What's with that man?' Lilla asks on the road from Rome to Assisi. Years before, Marco and she had a long argument, over plates of gnocchi and glasses of white wine at Riccarda's table, about the architectural politics of the South Bank and the Hayward Gallery where Lilla was exhibiting her sculptures. 'It's a concrete rabbit hutch,' he'd said, 'the living prison of culture.' At one point,

Mehran thought she was going to throw her glass of wine in his face. Then she'd seen him after years the night before, when he came to pick Mehran up from the café at the corner near her flat. 'He seems tormented. So much anger. And envy. Or jealousy. Something left unsaid between you? He looked so … confrontational.'

Guilt, Mehran thinks on the slow drive out of Rome, often makes the guilty offend the innocent.

'What exactly does "*ti voglio bene*" mean, Lilla?'

'You know what it means. You have to love someone to say it. Why do you ask?'

How close Marco was to me that Italian summer, twelve years ago. I wanted to tell you then, dear R, and I want to tell Lilla now, but I won't: let's leave it all in the past. He came so close I was able to let my joy, my passion for you, spill over into our friendship, and reliving that joy in words, or in his silent company, nearly doubled the pleasure of my yearning. He took me to Bracciano and Frascati and we talked and talked and sometimes we didn't say a word; we climbed hills, and played childish spitting games in ancient Etruscan cemeteries or in the Ostian Sea. Then, at some uncertain moment, we let it all slip away, the companionship and the conversations and the wordless tenderness. Or maybe I was the one to let it go. I remember how we struggled once, he and I, on a hot Roman evening by the riverbank in the shadow of Sant'Angelo, to translate those words of Shauq that ended 'The Poison of Love': 'Ishq men hamne ye kamaai ki/dil diya gham se aashnai ki.' I came up with something like this: 'For love's labour, this is what I earned/My heart I traded/and the craft of grief I learned.' And Marco laughed and said, 'But all it means is: "Questi sono i miei guadagni dell'amor / Ho dato il cuore e conosciuto il dolor." So much easier in Italian!' His rendition really was much closer to the bare music of the original.

'It's what Riccarda said to me when she came out from anesthesia. "*Ti voglio bene, amore mio.*" Didn't I ever tell you?'

Then, driving in the pale sunshine past Umbrian fields on that trip to Assisi, Mehran tells Lilla, as he tried to tell Marco the night before, how he had recounted, on another drive, in another season, another chapter of his story and Marvi's to Riccarda, and he must have shuddered while he told it because Riccarda said: 'Don't flinch like that. Have you ever thought that in some way you might have hurt her – might still be hurting her – as badly as you feel she hurt you? Let her go, Mehran, let her go.'

V

Dye my Scarf Green

Would that I could go home again,
to the land of my father's toil
that I might return to Malir
and die in the blooming desert soil

From 'Marvi's Song', Shah Abdul Latif

1994

One rainy February night, I came across a card in the library catalogue that may, I thought, lead me to my great-uncle Rafi's book of stories. I knew that an acquaintance of his called Rais Jaipuri had been entrusted with his manuscripts. Some of these, it was rumoured, may have disappeared, or were published anonymously. Rais had, however, edited a hefty collection of Rafi's work which was published after he died, with the title he had chosen himself: *Kehkashan.* But Rafi was an erasure: he wasn't even given a footnote in the books of literary history.

Now, under Rais Jaipuri's name where it had been erroneously catalogued and shelved, I managed to find the book. It was in the dustiest part of the library's basement. I photocopied the entire volume. Thus I finally discovered the work of the writer who might have influenced me earlier if I'd had a chance to read him. But before I began to read I wanted to take the photocopy as a gift to my mother. (My parents had moved to Kent in 1990, to be near their grandchildren; I bought their St John's Wood flat, lived there alone, and often took a train on Saturdays to spend twenty-four hours with them.) Though she had rarely spoken about her uncle, my mother was excited and touched, and when I gave her the xerox she told me more about him than she ever had. I was moved to learn how much my grandmother had missed her youngest brother: she had called one of her granddaughters, my sister Sara's first child, Kehkashan.

'Mamu Mian's stories should be translated,' my mother told me on the phone some weeks later.

'I'd love to, Ma. If only I could take some time off from my teaching.'

I was planning to be in London for most of the Easter weekend. For three days over the break I lost myself in Rafi's stories: I was late for a dinner on Saturday, and on Sunday I cancelled a visit to Canterbury, stayed home and read. Rafi's style was lucid, luminous, occasionally elaborate, sprinkled with the Persian words and syntax with which he was familiar. Far from being archaic, his realistic fiction was set in the increasingly modern milieu of his own time. It barely touched on the princely India into which his sister had married. He wrote about students and young men looking for their fortunes. Unlike the story I read in Delhi, much of his writing was deeply sympathetic to women: to young women with degrees and girls forced to look for jobs. The prevailing tone of his stories was light, witty and romantic. And given to happy endings.

Would he, had he lived, have become a fellow traveller of the leftist writers and progressives? His late stories showed an increasing awareness of, and sensitivity to, the nuances of class and the economics of marriage, I thought. But he died at thirty-three: six years younger than I was at the time I was reading him.

'I'll do them. At least a draft,' my mother said over lunch in her garden on Easter Monday.

She made a start right then, and posted me a handwritten draft of a story four days later, about a young woman working for a film company who found her lost love by inadvertently sending out a message in the subtitle of a silent film. It was called 'If You Love Me, Tell Me'. A month later, she posted me about fifty pages of handwritten manuscript, with the title 'Love's Call' written in bold capitals, in her beautiful copperplate.

My mother, I thought, was a better and far quicker translator than I would ever become.

I spent an entire Sunday on the joyous text she had produced, putting it on a disk. I had just replaced my electric typewriter with an Amstrad I inherited from Sara, who insisted that I enter the cyber age.

1995

I turned forty.

Lilla phoned with birthday greetings. She said a friend of hers in Venice was guest-editing an issue of a journal on postcolonial writing.

'I want an essay from you. Or a translation.'

'I don't have anything.'

'There was that story you wrote about Riccarda?'

I had almost forgotten. I had begun to write down all my memories of Riccarda a year after she died. I had thought I would try a sequence of prose poems, but what emerged instead was the story, in the plainest prose, of how we met at university and of the years I'd known her. Marco played a walk-on part. So did Marvi.

I had showed it only to Lilla, who felt I should do something with it, though she told me it was skeletal: too reticent, for example, about my passionate involvement with Riccarda and the long, lost months of loneliness that followed. I wanted to destroy it then, but instead I put away the typescript in the same old drawer in my bedside table and forgot about it.

I sent it back to her now, with some amendments and revisions. It was published as fiction.

1996

In summer, I visited Pakistan for the first time in twenty-seven years. I had edited and introduced a book of seven of Rafi's stories, four of them translated by my mother and three by me; it had come out there the year before, with a preface by the novelist Qurratulain Hyder. Later, I published a revised version of my childhood memories in a well-distributed Islamabad journal and, in Urdu translation, in a Karachi quarterly. I spoke about all that, and gave lectures on literature and on translation. 'What is the relevance of light, romantic writing like Rafi Ajmeri's to our lives today?' the veteran litterateur who was chairing my session asked. 'The elegance of his prose and its gorgeous irreverence: we could do with some irony in literary studies,' I retorted. 'The writing of his contemporaries is often so earnest.'

After visiting Islamabad and Lahore I returned to Karachi to rest for a few days before taking my flight back to London. Somehow I was less than surprised when Marvi, who hadn't attended any of my lectures though somewhere in my mind I thought she might, rang me from the café below the apartment block I was visiting in Zamzama, as if it hadn't been five years and more since we parted. It was raining, muddy, flood weather. For several hours, sometimes a day at a time, there was no electricity, and the streets were flooded. I remembered one summer it rained this way. I was eleven, my mother was in hospital, and crossing the flooded city in a hired car to visit her was a hazard. But I wasn't in search of my childhood here: it was the tense, crowded present of my native city that intrigued me, enthralled me. I thought Karachi had forgotten me but it claimed me back as if I'd never been too far, even if I had stayed away too long.

'Hey, you brought the thunder clouds with you, and London rain.'

Marvi grinned, and it seemed that the five years we were apart had just fallen, one by one, like pages off the calendar.

We talked all day, about ourselves and about the country. But mostly we talked about my trip, and about our work. She had been reading a lot too, and was doing some journalism and some translations. She had worked for a publisher cousin, editing a bilingual anthology of Parveen Shakir's poems, and while revising the inadequate English renditions she was inspired to read the Urdu. I told her I had dismissed Shakir for years as a lyricist who could only write about the pleasure and the malady of love, but when she died in a freak automobile accident in 1994, the obituaries forced me to look at her work again. 'I wrote about her when she died,' Marvi said. 'I remember I'd read a few poems of hers when I was about twenty and loved them then. When I read her I just wish my Urdu was good enough to write in!'

The discipline of Shakir's syntax and the almost Persian grace of her complex vocabulary drew me to her verses; something else in her voice – a yearning, vulnerable intimacy beyond technique, born of our time and our generation – spoke to Marvi. (And there were verses that could have been about our relationship: 'We ought to have met/in a kinder age/in the hope of a dream/in another sky/in another land.')

But it was Shakir's broken marriage, her life as a single mother, her charisma, and most of all her early death that Marvi was drawn to.

'She'd done so much at that young age. She didn't reach her forty-second birthday. Look at me, I've done nothing yet, and I'm not even going to live to see forty.'

Marvi had almost given up drinking, but was still depending on painkillers to see her through everything.

She dropped me off, too late for dinner, at the house of the aunt I was staying with in Clifton, near the sea.

1997

August. Marvi moved back to London and into a flat across the road from me, at the corner of Lisson Grove. When they divorced, her husband and she had sold the Clifton Hill house and she bought the new flat with her share of the money. She said Karachi had become a place of vigilantes and random vandalism, and even Bath Island, where she had always lived, was no longer safe enough for a woman on her own with children. And after Murtaza Bhutto had been shot down on the streets she lost all hope in the new government. She put her boys in boarding school in Scotland and made her way back to London.

She was thirty-eight; I was forty-two. I taught long hours at the university. I spent a lot of time alone, reading or listening to music. Most winters I travelled, to escape the sting of London's cold, to India or Bangladesh or Java; I could afford to, now that I had a Reader's post. I had learned that most people lived for work or their families, and since I didn't want to do either I thought that at least I could see other landscapes, other skies.

On autumn evenings I came back from my classes and walked over to Marvi's place. She was planning a new book, on neo-liberal economics in what were now called the developing countries; she had a particular interest in the Emirates. Both of us were disappointed in Blair, as we'd been disappointed in Benazir a few years before; I still marched and signed petitions, though I had put all my political hopes on hold. Sitting shoulder to shoulder, holding hands like children with all desire spent and the familiarity of old lovers dangling like a cobweb between us, Marvi and I would listen to Noor Jehan's songs, singing along with them, or we would recite, in exaggerated imitations of romantic poets in performance at a symposium, verses we remembered by heart. Sometimes we read to each other from Shakir, or other books of poems we had brought back from Pakistan, that jagged free verse our contemporaries were writing and I had learned to understand.

But best of all Marvi loved the great poets of eighteenth-century Sindh, Shah Abdul Latif and Sachal Sarmast. She remembered how, as a child, she heard travelling musicians, on their way back from a festival at some shrine, singing these songs at her grandfather's gate; sometimes they were called in to perform, and the women of the house listened from behind a curtain, but her grandfather allowed her to sit beside him, to listen to them sing, until she was eleven. On a shelf in her grandfather's house, she had discovered a signed translation into English of Shah Abdul Latif's *Risalo*, by Elsa Kazi, a German woman who had married a Sindhi scholar in the early years of the century and spent most of her life in her husband's country, writing poems and stories. She gave me the book as a gift.

Marvi would dream of the heroines of Latif's stories, brave, tragic women, often of peasant background, who set out in search of lost loves and died along the way. She had borrowed her name from one of them. I, too, had grown up listening to singers perform the saint-poet's beautiful song-like poems since childhood, and had even tried to read the originals with the aid of Urdu versions. But now, Marvi and I would read the poems together while we listened to them, sung by Abida Parveen and others. Because she knew the language of the originals, I came closer to understanding the rapture of the verses: laments for lost loves, but also celebrations of the desert and the clouds and the rainy season.

Marvi showed me a typescript of a translation :

My cloud-friend's playing rain music
I dye my scarf rice-green
I hang bells around my little calf's neck

I dye my scarf rice-green
Latif says: Come to my courtyard
Take care of me, friend
I'll dye my scarf rice-green

It was from Latif's *Sur Sarang*, but when I asked her who had done it, she said she didn't know.

Kazi's renditions, which attempted to replicate the elliptical cadences of Latif's songs, were compelling, but to my ear they did not always work as poems. I spent hours one Wednesday afternoon in the library, looking up every translation I could find, and took the volumes I borrowed over to Marvi's. We planned for a while to translate some of the great poet's work into English, but between Marvi's brief attention span and my commitments, we never found the time. Only later – much later – I realised Marvi had translated the song about dyeing the scarf rice-green, probably on some stormy Karachi afternoon.

Marvi was shrunken and skeletal, her eyes huge and leaf-brown in her little wax-lantern skull. 'I look like Morticia Adams,' she groaned when she caught casual sight of herself in a mirror. She almost always went out in a wheelchair: if she took too many steps without a stick, she fell. She had arranged for a young Javanese divorcee to look after her; Sumirah spoke good English and looked after her well, cooking and keeping the flat tidy. The rumour was that during her years in Karachi Marvi was sniffing cocaine. She had come back to London to escape from the habit into the relative ease of prescription drugs. I had learned not to ask her more than she told me. She'd been a part of me I'd torn out long ago, a part I never understood, or even admitted to losing, but still I felt a pain like an amputation of a limb when she left. Now that I had ceased to feel that pain, I could care for her from a distance.

During the years in which I'd been teaching and travelling and writing, she went through something painful in Karachi that I could only guess at. She had put a distance between herself and not just me but the hunger, the thirst, the craving she'd had for life, for love. And that distance made an equal affection, or what seemed like one, easier for us both.

Marvi had discovered the kind of solitude that had always been my companion. She would spend hours reading, listening to music, drawing, writing. I hoped that she, too, would find a form to work in, a new form to contain her musings. Even in our most tender and companionable moments I could sometimes sense her withdrawing from our conversation – her eyes would wander, her sentences dangle incomplete. At first I thought the painkillers were doing that. Now it was I who sometimes wanted to stay with her a little longer, to ward off the night for another hour or two before I crossed the road and switched on the lights and the television in my own flat. But soon I knew it was not me she was withdrawing from, but every one of her memories, of joy, of pain. And when her eyelids began to droop and her voice grew faint I would kiss her forehead and leave.

I remembered how she had once said: 'Pain, that's all there is. You think it's love, but it's only pain.' We spent our youth looking for signs in the night; for a while, each one of us thought the other was that sign, and when we found how wrong we were we looked for light elsewhere. Now we knew that the night's darkness, the solitude and absence it offered us, together and apart, was the sign we had been looking for.

Once she kissed the tips of my fingers and said: 'Who'll be there for you when I'm gone? How can I leave you alone? I don't even have anyone to tell to keep an eye on you. You don't eat properly. You starve yourself all day and then you stuff yourself with bread and rice. You're careless about your health. You chain-smoke.'

I put my head in her lap. 'Don't be morbid.'

Then she told me that if she did live on another year or two, I should stay with her, maybe even marry her.

At other times she'd turn her head away from me and say we never would have made it, she and

I, even if she had been whole and well. 'We met too late. Or too early.'

Beneath another sky. In another land. How tender she could be then. Many years ago, she sent me a Valentine: *Mehran and Marvi/Sitting on a tree/K-I-S-S-I-N-G,* with a sketch of stick figures and a tree, and a pierced heart scribbled below that, which she had coloured a deep scarlet. I might have thought it sentimental, but I remembered how I'd told her about a little girl who'd written that in my autograph book when I was ten, and I laughed. 'But trust you, Marvi, to over-egg the cake with the heart.' 'Oh, your mixed metaphors!' she protested.

On a summer evening Marvi said: 'I've become a liar: I lie all the time to doctors to get my painkillers. I make my friends lie. I feel like a thief. I fought Umar for custody of the boys and now I seldom see them. They're better away from me. But if it weren't for the thought of seeing them I'd just jump out of the window. I can't live like this any more.'

1998

Late January. She was in hospital: we were only allowed to see her with plastic gloves on. She was wired to all sorts of contraptions and bottles. She smiled when I walked in, and soon seemed to fall into a gentle sleep. Then she took away the piece that covered her mouth and spoke.

'Marco ...'

'Mehran, Marvi. It's me. Mehran.'

'I know it's you, darling. I just want to tell you I only stopped seeing Marco two years ago. He even visited me in Karachi. He wanted me to tell you that. But after that I never saw him again. When he calls I want you to say ...'

I didn't know what unresolved fantasies her mind was replaying.

'Rest, darling.'

Against hospital rules, I squeezed the hand she extended in my gloved hand, and took it to my cheek.

'Love you lots. Don't leave ...'

'Me too. Now go back to sleep. I'm not leaving.'

'Forgive ...?' Her voice was weak, and slurred.

'Nothing to forgive,' I said. I think I meant it.

Dear R,

Years ago, one of the last times I saw you, you told me a fable by a Senegalese sage, about all men being like walls full of holes in which birds nested, white birds and black, ravens and doves. 'If you send out the white birds to someone else they return to their nests with blessings, but the ravens of rancour are always in search of empty spaces to occupy and will pick holes in the wall they perch on. Don't send your ravens to anyone.' I can't remember exactly when, but one day I told Marvi your story.

Your loving M.

On the last evening of the year, Marvi rang to ask what I was doing. She was on her way to dinner at a friend's.

'I've got a chest infection, Marvi. I'm in my dressing gown. I've cancelled an outing. These years that come and go don't seem to matter much any more.'

'Well, maybe see you ... tomorrow then?'

I had been asked to give a talk on performative modes in South Asian poetry at the University of Leeds, at a conference that would fall on the Persian New Year; I thought I would write about the Indus tradition for once, rather than the ubiquitous *ghazal* or *masnavi*. I was trying to revise and put in order the notes I had made. For background noise, I switched the TV on to a cable channel that was playing videos of mellow jazz performances, Carmen McRae and Thelonious Monk and others, vocal and instrumental. Listening to them, I noticed again how American blues singers sang from the same raw places as our folk musicians.

Persian remained a language of courtiers, I read in my notebook, *while the vast majority of the populace spoke their vernaculars. The cosmopolitan tradition of Persian was fragmented by the rise of poetry in local languages. In India, Urdu replaced Persian as the favoured language of poets, although little Sufi poetry of note was written in Urdu until the appearance of Iqbal in the twentieth century. In many parts of South Asia, more and more poets turned to vernacular dialects to sing their songs and tell their tales ... the lessons of the Persian masnavi had, however, been well learned and adapted to indigenous needs; folk heroes and heroines, Sassi and Punnu and Heer and Ranjha, Momal and Rano and Umar and Marvi brought their poems closer, in characterisation and landscape, to readers and listeners. In the lands of the Indus, great poets were to emerge, creating new traditions: Waris Shah and Bulle Shah in the Punjab, Shah Abdul Latif and Sachal Sarmast in the Sindh. Bulle and Latif were both born in the 1680s, and helped to propagate an indigenised Sufism that appealed to common people of all religions. Language, particularly in the case of Bulle, can be rough; form, for both, serves as a performative element. Latif was a skilled musician who set his own verses to music. The work of both poets is meant to be declaimed or sung. These song-poems are called kafi in the Punjab, and wai in the Sindh, terms that refer more to their performative function than to their prosody, which allows the poet more technical freedom than the innate courtliness of Persian or Urdu. Metaphors and similes, too, are bucolic. Cotton-seed, harvest, village fair are used as emblems of life, in its struggles and regenerations. The humble spinning wheel and the butter churn become symbols of the business of living. Take, for example, Abdul Latif, the most sung and celebrated of Sindhi poets, who, in his Sur Sarang ('Rain Song'), wrote about the rainfall on the Thar desert ...*

> *Today, too, there are hopes of rain,*
> *the clouds are dark and low,*
> *o friends, with monsoons, longing for*
> *the loved one comes again.*

The rain pours on the desert sands,
on hills and vales around,
at early dawn we rise to hear
the churn's soft, humming sound.

The cloud, with colours rich and bright,
paints towers in the skies,
brings zither, violin, tambour
and flute, to give delight.

Herdsmen's wives about their necks
of blossoms garlands wind,
cucumbers, mushrooms, vegetables,
fruit of every kind.

I hope the rain will water well
the parched and longing plain.
Beloved, come! my life sustain,
all seasons turn to spring.

I was immersed in Latif's words and Elsa Kazi's translations, from which I was choosing excerpts, when, at nine, the doorbell rang. I marked my page with the peacock feather Marvi had placed in the book, went to the door, and there she was: wrapped up in a great beige cape in a wheelchair pushed by Sumirah, the Javanese carer. Her eyes were lined with kohl, her lips ruby-red; her face, nestling in a hood, had some of its prior glamour. She had brought me two brown paper bags full of my favourite Persian food, lamb kebabs and buttery rice and yoghurt with dill and hot bread fresh from the oven, and though she didn't share the meal, she sat and watched me eat.

'Hey, I've been looking at that book you gave me, the Kazi translations. Weren't we supposed to rework some of those poems?'

'We can do it at the seaside, when it's warmer. Next year! Let's hope it's a better one. Do you know anyone who might want to rent my flat? I'm moving to Brighton this month,' she said. 'I'm happiest by the sea. It takes me back to Karachi.'

Soon after eleven, she went off in her wheelchair to see the old year out with her friends.

I left the curtains undrawn and watched fireworks light up the London sky.

1999

A few days before her birthday in April, she phoned to invite me to celebrate with her in Brighton. The day before the party, Sumirah called to say: 'Come over immediately, she's in and out of a coma, she asked for you this morning.' I thought it was one of Marvi's jokes, but it was true: she'd kept her word, about not living to see forty.

Memory: Marvi dancing. Dressed in black. The fragile wrists. And then the fall.

Marvi died six years to the month (and almost to the day) after Riccarda. I saw her face, almost free of pain, one final time, at the mosque where we read funeral prayers before they flew her coffin to Sindh, to bury her in the cemetery by the ancient shrine where her ancestors lay.

Marvi, Riccarda. My night guests, my dream visitors who died at dawn. Interred in the twentieth century. We are born, we die, and sometimes, for a while, we do something in between. Sometimes we live as though we were dead, or we die while we're living. Most often, though, our lives are just a sequence of bookends, afterthoughts, epilogues.

As I walked away from the mosque towards the station, I saw two gulls wheeling overhead in a blanched and naked sky, and I wondered what had brought them to town on such a dry day, to a place where there was no water. I tried to remember whether the Thames flowed nearby. I was sure it didn't. My footsteps were unburdened but my eyes felt like drifting clouds full of rain and undelivered messages.

I left for my first trip to New York a day or two after Marvi's funeral.

VI

Berries and Fruits of the Land

There were deserts between us.
But now, the desert is green.
The rain of grace fell
and we eat
berries and fruits of the land.

Annemarie Schimmel, 'Marui in Umarkot'

2010

'Your camel-racing professor! She lived to be ninety-six, you know,' Lilla says. 'She died last July.'

'Lady L? Last summer? No! Surely she's been dead for ages?'

It's April. They're smoking by a fountain in the courtyard of an old church Lilla wants Mehran to see. Talking about Riccarda in the rain. (Years ago, Lilla guided Riccarda into Lady L's classes, though she's never told me why.)

They look it up on Lilla's iPhone; Lilla's right, Lady L retired to the northern town where she was born, and had a late flowering as a fire-breathing evangelist in the local parish church. She also fulminated against migrants in the green and pleasant land, quoting an old friend in the Himalayas who said his kingdom had remained safe for centuries because they had never allowed foreigners to settle there. The obituaries confirmed the rumours about her activities in the world of espionage and political skullduggery. But unlike the shock of so many death notices, when you discover someone you once knew or cared for has been gone a while without your knowing, the only surprise this time was her late-blooming religious mission, and that she had lived on for so many years.

'So weren't you afraid to go there – amidst all the bombs?'

'I'm more annoyed by security at airports these days. I was going home, after all.'

Mehran had come to Rome from Karachi several days ago, to celebrate Lilla's seventieth birthday, which fell on May Day. It was marked by the presentation to her of a *festschrift* at a conference on the poetics of translation. He hasn't been back for seventeen years, since that last trip to Assisi. Now it's nearly time for him to leave.

They're having farewell drinks in that Trastevere flat Mehran first stayed in with Riccarda; Lilla and her long-time companion Flavio have invited over a group of friends and academic colleagues they want him to meet.

Of all of them, Lilla has possibly traversed time best. Her once-spare body is imposing now, her long blonde hair a white rain cloud. She has her grandchild, her garden, the wounded animals that come to her for shelter. She carves in driftwood; she says time's too short for working with stone. She lives in the country and only comes to Rome for moments of what she calls digression. But she writes her poetry too, and translates Khusrau, Mirabai, Kabir and Shah Abdul Latif into Italian.

Lilla, Mehran reflects, lives life like a continuous prelude.

An archaelogist friend of hers is talking about a man called Marco, who spends six months of the year leading workshops on spiritual self-development in Delhi, where he lives in a flat beside Humayun's tomb, and the other six on an Umbrian farm, from which he emerges occasionally to teach a seminar at some institute in Rome. He's apparently had a succession of partners, and a couple of children with different mothers.

'Marco who?'

'Marco Feliciani ...'

Yes, it's him. My friend, my rival.

'I told him to join us tonight,' Flavio says. 'He rang to say he was held up at the airport this afternoon, a cancelled flight, adverse weather, an ash cloud from some Icelandic volcano, he said: he's on his way now from Milan, he took a train, should be here in just a while. Your name seemed to register with him. Do you know him? He was in London – oh, years ago, says he studied with Professor Lambert too, graduated around the same time ...'

'I remember him. We weren't in the same year for Persian.'

Apparently Marco has made a lot of successful documentaries about Sufi shrines all over the world, and is now writing a book about the relationship of Bergson and Iqbal's Persian poems. He's seen as something of a Sufi philosopher in certain circles, not a convert to Islam, but an advocate of Schuon and Burckhardt and their theories of the essential oneness of all faith and of eternal knowledge. He must, at some point, have resurrected his Persian. Or, knowing him, he probably acquired a willing apprentice to do the hard work for him. I wonder whether he ever forgave me for whatever it was that made him so angry with me, though I've long forgotten what it might have been.

'Lilla tells me you have a new book coming out here soon, an autobiographical novel.' A stranger approaches him.

'That's an exaggeration. Just a handful of reflections. Impressions of people and places. I guess you could call them fictions. All Lilla's fault. She collected them from here and there, slung them together and gave them to Flavio, who's starting a publishing company with a group of colleagues ...'

Mehran pauses, and wonders whether anyone will recognise them, Riccarda and even Lilla, and if Marco will read it. But Lilla says he shouldn't worry, it was all so long ago, and in any case he's changed all the names, even his own.

'What's the book called?'

I wanted a title that echoed the rain. The sounds of gulls crying, a dead flute. And I like the story my mother told of a cloud carrying messages of love across landscapes. On a plane to Karachi one morning, I randomly opened that old translation of Latif's Risalo Marvi gave me and came upon the Sur Sarang, those lyrics about clouds and the rainfall on the desert, marked with the peacock feather she left in it. That afternoon, my friend Nada played me a recording of a Sindhi wai: it was one of the Songs of Marvi. After those signs, I knew my title.

Mehran pours himself some water, lights a cigarette.

'I haven't decided.'

He smiles and turns away.

Author's Note

In May 1978, a few weeks after my twenty-third birthday, I walked out of the bank where I had been working, on the final day of my training as a junior officer. I had no clear idea of where I was going next.

I had always been curious about Middle Eastern Studies, and arranged to meet the heads of both Persian and Turkish at SOAS that summer, but was told I would have to make a choice. I chose Persian because I knew the script and I could also study Urdu literature along with it.

My university years were not the most eventful or significant of my life. My primary interest was in world music. In my final year, I was busier with French linguistic and cultural studies, which I did at the same time as I prepared for my degree. Three years after leaving SOAS, I went on to study psychoanalysis and philosophy, and embarked on a dissertation on Lacan, Klein and Sartre. In 1987, I published my first short story, 'The Colour of a Loved Person's Eyes', and left behind my dissertation (and academe) to become a working writer in the London of the late eighties.

My professional life was to be dedicated to the English language. But in the nineties, my abandoned interest in Urdu literature resurfaced, and I began to realise what I had learned during the three years of study I had come to think of as lost, or at least forgotten.

My novel is the story of some of the paths I might have taken.

The characters and most of the situations here are imaginary.

The poets I quote are not.

Aamer Hussein
London, October 2010

Acknowledgements

I would like to thank Lynn Gaspard at Telegram, Bruno Lo Turco (my Italian editor and translator), and Dalu Jones for ideas that made a story, 'The Grammar of Grief', into this book; Shikha Sethi, my editor, for her interest and encouragement; Shirley Chew for publishing a chapter in *Moving Worlds*; Joseph Olshan for reading an early draft; Peter Middleton and Tabish Khair for responses to a later one; Bina Shah and Nada Raza for being there from the start; and Alev Adil for an illuminating reading of Mehran's character as I wrote him.

Most of the translations in the book are my own, but I have been aided in a couple of places by I.I. and Elsa Kazi's and Anne-Marie Schimmel's work on Shah Abdul Latif, and Ralph Russell on Mir. Finally, *Urdu Literature* by C.S. Shackle, David Matthews and Shahrukh Husain served to remind me of what I might have forgotten.

Read More

Aamer Hussein

ANOTHER GULMOHAR TREE

Shortlisted for the Commonwealth Writers' Prize Europe and South Asia 2010

Usman is visiting post-war London from Pakistan when he meets a young aspiring artist, Lydia, who has, like himself, come out of an unhappy marriage. Just as the lonely strangers' friendship begins to blossom into something deeper, Usman has to return to Karachi, leaving Lydia behind.

Two years later, Lydia impulsively abandons her life in London and boards a ship to Karachi, where the two are married. But as the years flit by, Usman feels distanced from his life and realises that he hasn't noticed the buds of the gulmohar tree unfurl.

'Aamer Hussein has the rare gift of expressing enduring and radiant happiness.' *Independent*

'Hussein vibrantly evokes the Karachi of the 1950s and 60s in an affectionate tribute to a long marriage.' *Guardian*

'Quiet voices sometimes find it difficult to be heard. Hussein gives great pleasure to those who listen carefully' *Daily Telegraph*

'Framed in distilled prose, this is a moving fable about the slow and sometimes startling growth of love. A slender delight.' *Financial Times*

Read More

Aamer Hussein

INSOMNIA

An elusive Japanese girl leads a teenage boy into a world of passion and conflict; in Andalusia, a man talks to his friend about longing and belonging; a translator finds himself drawn into the personal and political turmoil of the poet he translates; and a woman's quiet world is eroded by the onset of war and the movement for independence. Moving from Karachi to England, through India, Java, Italy and Spain, these exquisite stories engage with the grand narratives of our time.

'Profound but low key; spiritual, but pragmatic; full of longing, but also acceptance ... These stories feel like the work of an outsider – subtle expressions of alienation in which characters are frequently misunderstood, rarely heard and never feel a sense of belonging.' *Independent on Sunday*

'Superbly written short fiction ... Hussein's writing is full of strange and brilliant images, which seem utterly modern, but rooted in history and magic ... the writing is both delicate and powerful.' William Palmer, *Independent*

'Hussein is a sensuous writer in whose stories nature acts as a balm on even the most weary of sensibilities.' *Literary Review*

Read More

Aamer Hussein

TURQUOISE

Direct yet startlingly intimate, Hussein's stories are set in troubled times – in Karachi, Lahore and London, where war, partition and military rule form the backdrop for the anticipation and anxiety of changing homes and family life, the hopes and failures of love and work. *Turquoise* illuminates the passions and fears of a world far more complex and beautiful than the media images of Islam and Pakistan convey.

'One of the most significant and interesting writers of Pakistani English fiction.' Muneeza Shamsie

'*Turquoise* must be read slowly to savour its many pleasures ... The fluid prose is sometimes simple and pristine, sometimes sinuous and visceral ... The stories' imagery is radiant.' Mary Flanagan, *Independent*

'Hussein writes with the economy and skill of a poet ... romance, imagination and their capacity to make sense of the world are qualities found in abundance in his work.' James W. Wood, *TLS*

Aamer Hussein

THIS OTHER SALT

Betrayal, bereavement, exile, belonging – these are the themes that resonate throughout *This Other Salt*. A writer torn between two loves looks for his lost words in the gap between memory, mourning and desire; a poet takes revenge on her faithless lover by turning their romance into a legend of biblical proportions; and a teenage boy's life uncannily begins to resemble the role he plays in a school operetta. Combining satire, legend, poetry, history and memoir, the linked stories of *This Other Salt* reveal an author of uncommon talent at the height of his craft.

'Poetic perfection ... Drawing on legend, history, memoir, literature and film, Hussein's stories are meant to be cupped in both hands and savoured slowly, like a cup of cardamom chai.' *Guardian*

'Extraordinarily controlled, written in a tactile, musical prose, with a very individual sense of beauty ... A striking and genuinely original contribution ... a moving and highly aesthetic expression of a new sensibility.' Amit Chaudhuri

'Each story sings with heartbreak, intelligence and elegy. A stunning collection.' Kamila Shamsie